Chapter One

"I don't believe it!" Rocky slammed down the telephone.

"What is it? What's happened?" Katie, my little sister, was frantic.

We were all crowded in the kitchen: Sarah, our stepmother; my brother Ross; Danny, who was practically family; James, our vet; and Blake who was now a professional show-jumper.

I was perched on the edge of my seat. Katie was clinging on to her plastic four-leaf clover for good luck and Ross was pacing up and down.

"Well, don't keep us in suspense!" Sarah shouted. "What's going on?"

Rocky stood in the doorway, looking every inch a famous rock star. He was one of the best performers in the world and always on television and winning awards. His music was inspirational and his concerts sold out within hours. He was also one of the nicest people I'd ever met.

He was so down to earth it was incredible and his generosity was beyond question. What is more,

1

he was one of the biggest supporters of Hollywell Stables – our sanctuary for horses and ponies – and what he had created in the last few weeks was about to change our lives for ever. That is – if it worked!

"Rocky, for heaven's sake, tell us what's happened!" Sarah was practically shaking him by the shoulders.

At Christmas Rocky had announced that he was writing a song especially for Hollywell with all the royalties going to the sanctuary. We hadn't really believed he would go through with it and after the initial excitement we'd put it right out of our minds. So it had been like a bolt out of the blue when he rang up to say the song was finished and already recorded, and when could they shoot the video?

It had blown us away at first. We couldn't take it in. It was only when the TV cameras turned up to make the video that it finally dawned on us that this was for real. Even now I couldn't believe the short roll of film which everyone had worked around the clock to make was to be seen on television. Hollywell Stables could become a household name!

But Rocky's expression soon brought me crashing down to earth. He looked shell-shocked.

"It's bad news, isn't it?" Ross broke the silence.

Rocky had just been talking to his personal manager. The reason why we were all on tenterhooks was that today was the day when the record was released and we were waiting with baited breath to see if it had charted. If it was a success it could mean a new lease of life for Hollywell Stables – we would be able to buy more land, put up a new stable block, rescue more horses. The tension was unbearable and I didn't think I could stand it much longer.

"It's not bad news," Rocky suddenly blurted out. "It's made the charts!"

Katie and Danny leapt up screaming "yippee" and punching the air with their fists. Rocky broke into a wide grin, and Sarah threw the tea towel at him for keeping us in suspense.

"And there's more," Rocky shouted out, banging a spoon on the table to get everybody's attention. Blake and Ross were giving each other a high five and James was twirling Sarah round in the air. It was complete bedlam.

"Order, everybody, I've not finished," Rocky bellowed, trying to compete with Jigsaw, our golden Labrador, who was barking non-stop.

We all piped down and Rocky dropped his bombshell. Now I knew why he'd looked so shocked when he came off the telephone.

"It's gone straight in at Number Ten!" he yelled.

Chase the Dream is at Number Ten!"

It was a miracle. It was beyond belief. We all knew the record was good, but to go straight into the Top Ten . . .

"I told you it was a belter," Rocky smirked, pushing back his long jet black hair with the white streak down the middle and reaching for the chocolate biscuits. Sarah always joked that when Rocky came to stay we needed to buy choccy biscuits by the car-load. He devoured them like nobody's business but he was still as thin as a rake.

"You know what this means, don't you, Mel?" Ross ruffled my hair so it all stuck up on end. "We're going to be famous!"

It was the horses who were going to be famous, not us. They were what was important. The video had shown them out in the field, playing and sleeping, and the terrible pictures of when they'd first arrived, all too often thin and starving and on the verge of death. We all thought the words to the song were deeply moving and Rocky had decided to call it *Chase the Dream* because that's exactly what we were all doing – chasing an ideal, achieving the impossible, trying to create a world without cruelty or neglect.

The next few days were chaotic. The telephone

never stopped ringing. We had scores of well-wish-ers wanting to know how they could help and one of the Sunday papers wanted to do a centre-page spread on how Rocky had become involved with the sanctuary. It was awe-inspiring and it totally bowled us over.

It seemed a lifetime ago since Ross had posted off a letter to America asking if Rocky would do a concert in our village hall to raise money for Hollywell. It had been a long shot and none of us expected a reply, let alone a personal visit from Rocky himself. As it turned out, he not only did the concert, despite having fractured ribs, but moved into Hollywell, bought us a horsebox, spent Christmas day with us and helped us rescue a racehorse called Dancer and his own horse, Ter-ence, from the corrupt stables where they were both kept. Rocky said we had to go on radio and give interviews and even Ross was petrified at the thought of it. None of us had been prepared for the attention and publicity *Chase the Dream* would give us. Without Rocky to guide us through it, I don't think any of us would have been able to cope.

"Mel! Blake! Quick – in the house!" Ross came charging into the yard as soon as Blake and I rode up on Colorado and Royal Storm. Blake was staying with us for the Easter holidays while his own stables were being renovated. He'd brought along his three show-jumpers and we'd just been for a quiet hack along the country lanes.

"Come on, you two, hurry up!" Ross grabbed hold of Colorado's reins and pushed us both towards the house where it sounded as if a party was in full swing and it was only ten o'clock in the morning!

I pulled off my riding hat and pushed open the door and Sarah immediately dived towards me, looking ecstatic. Sarah, our stepmother, had become our very best friend since our dad had died a few years ago, and long before that our real mother had abandoned us to live abroad with another man. Sarah meant everything to us and without her we would never have set up Hollywell Stables.

"You'll never guess what's happened, in a million years!" Katie chanted, as precocious as ever.

Rocky came across, unable to keep the secret any longer. "We've just heard from *The Breakfast Bunch* team," he started.

The Breakfast Bunch was the main Saturday morning children's programme and the one which everybody was talking about.

"They want to cover the story," Rocky went on. "They're sending their own film crew tomorrow morning to get started!"

Chapter Two

We'd had local film crews at Hollywell before, but never anything like this. They completely took the place over!

Two estate cars, with *The Breakfast Bunch* written down the side in bold letters, powered into the yard and from that moment onwards it was chaos.

The producer introduced himself as Dominic and swanned around as if he'd just stepped out of a Hollywood stage set. He wore a bright green bow tie and patterned waistcoat and kept shouting out things like, "It's a wrap, it's a wrap!"

His assistant, Cassandra, was no less affected and looked like a gangly giraffe at the side of him. She permanently had a clipboard in her hand and a pen stuck in her mouth and kept saying "Ya" instead of "Yes" and calling everybody "sweetie" and "darling". Sarah could hardly keep a straight face and said she would have to use Dominic and Cassandra as inspiration for her next book. Sarah was a romantic novelist and she was always scribbling down ideas for future storylines.

Katie and Danny were in seventh heaven, especially when one of the crew lifted a camera on to their shoulders. Danny couldn't believe how heavy it was and went deathly pale when he was told how much it cost.

The first hour's filming was a complete disaster as Boris, our black hunter, devoured the furry sound device which looked like someone's wig and Jigsaw kept running in front of the camera as soon as it started rolling. Ross said he wanted to be famous too.

The Breakfast Bunch wanted to make a twenty-minute film on Hollywell to be put out on next Saturday's three-hour show. They also wanted us in the studio to answer questions from the audience. Just the idea of it brought me out in a heat rash, and Blake looked positively ill when Dominic said he was included and he wanted him to talk about Colorado and how he had gone on to become a top-class show-jumper.

Cassandra was horrified when she accidentally put her hand in a wheelbarrow of horse muck, and insisted on wearing gloves at all times from then on. Dominic kept asking if we could arrange a rescue so they could film it all happening live and we had to explain that cases didn't just pop up to order. Sometimes it was months before we took in another horse and then we might have a run of quite a few.

At lunchtime they all cleared off to the pub and left us gasping for breath and a few moments' peace and quiet. That's when we noticed that Rocky's huge white limousine was missing and there was a note pinned up on the back door: "Gone to Lake District. Back soon."

"What does he think he's playing at?" Ross was horrified.

I was scared stiff. We were due to do a phone-in programme at the local radio station in approximately three hours. How could we cope without Rocky?

"What's he up to in the Lake District?" Sarah mused, folding over the piece of paper thoughtfully.

"Whatever it is, it's got to be important," Ross added. "He wouldn't run out on us for nothing. It's got to be really serious."

For once I agreed with my brother. It wasn't Rocky's style to disappear like this. It had to be something important. The question was, what? We didn't have much time to find out.

As soon as the TV crew returned we had to rush off to the radio station, leaving Danny and Katie with Mrs Mac to listen to the broadcast. Sarah, Ross, Blake and myself were doing the show and as we were led from the reception to the studio my heart was beating so loudly I wondered how I'd hear what the presenter was saying, let alone the callers. My stomach physically hurt with nerves and the tasteless cup of black coffee one of the researchers had given me didn't make me feel any better.

Sarah clutched my arm as we went into the studio, where a man wearing glasses was fiddling with switches. It all looked so complicated. We were shown to some seats around a table with a mike and I was horrified when I saw the earphones which Rocky had told me were called cans. They were huge.

Blake squeezed my hand under the table and I immediately felt better. Ever since I'd first met Blake, when he'd been a groom for a girl called Louella, he'd always been there for me, a solid rock, a best friend. I didn't think I'd be able to get through this without him.

The red light saying "On Air" lit up and I could hear *Chase the Dream* being played through the earphones. I tried to remember what Rocky had told us: take deep breaths, wait for the presenter to finish talking, don't babble on and don't think about the thousands of people listening!

"Here in the studio this afternoon we have the family responsible for setting up Hollywell Stables to which *Chase the Dream* is dedicated. We'll be opening the phone lines in just a second, but first a few questions . . ."

My mouth felt so dry I could barely speak. Sarah started to do the talking and then Ross joined in, but I just sat there like a dummy and clung to Blake's hand as if it was my last link with life.

"And just whose idea was it to write to Rocky?"

Ross started to explain how he'd seen an article in a magazine about Rocky owning a racehorse and it had developed from there. Sarah admitted she hadn't been keen on the idea but now she thought Rocky was the best person in the world and *Chase the Dream* was truly brilliant. Ross nudged her arm to get her to shut up and I spilt the remains of my coffee all over my jeans.

"Also linked to the sanctuary, we have with us up and coming show-jumper Blake Kildaire who has been tipped for a European medal next autumn. Tell me, Blake, is it true you've become a bit of a pin-up with the ladies?"

Blake went bright red in the face and squeezed my hand so tightly my fingers nearly dropped off. I had to kick his ankle to get him to say something.

"And of course we've all heard of the remarkable Colorado, the half-wild Mustang, who was rescued by the sanctuary, but just how did you save his life, Mel?"

I totally froze. I couldn't say a thing. My mouth was just gaping open and shut but nothing came out. Blake leapt in to save me as usual and once he started talking about Colorado he couldn't shut up, but the presenter loved every minute of it.

"That's an amazing story, Blake, and who knows, maybe one day an Olympic medal?"

And then the phone lines opened. This was actually easier than answering the presenter's questions because at least you couldn't see the caller's face. It was just like talking on the phone but into a microphone instead.

I actually managed to answer a couple of questions on how many horses we'd rescued and what we were planning to do with the money from *Chase the Dream*.

Ross got completely carried away talking about Queenie and how we'd saved her from starvation in a scrapyard, and then Sarah answered a more difficult question about whether we got used to seeing cases of cruelty and did it get any easier.

That wasn't a simple one to answer because of course every case was distressing, but it wasn't quite so shocking as it had been in the beginning. You got used to seeing animals in terrible condition.

There were scores of callers, mainly young girls, wanting to know how to join the Hollywell Stables

Fan Club and the presenter said he'd give out the address at the end of the show. Then he put on a record and congratulated us on our first performance. I realized that it was now safe to talk without being heard by the listeners and took my first deep breath since coming into the studio.

Then the researcher came in looking extremely agitated. He whispered something to the presenter who nodded thoughtfully and filled us in on the problem. There was a young girl on one of the lines, desperately trying to get through. She wanted to tell us about a pony in a caravan or something. She'd spotted it while she'd been walking her dog.

"Put her through," Sarah was adamant. "We've got to hear what she has to say."

The record finished and any fear I'd had about being on the radio had suddenly disappeared. This was far more serious. There was a life at stake. How could anybody fit a pony into a caravan?

The voice came through sounding young and scared. She wouldn't give her name, she hardly spoke in more than a whisper.

"Listen, luv, can you speak up a little? We can hardly hear you." The presenter gently coaxed her, all the time trying to keep her on the line, not wanting her to hang up. "What's all this about a pony?"

There was a long silence. We could hear a dog

barking in the background and the television blaring out.

"Are you still there?" The presenter sounded anxious.

"We're here to help," Sarah tried. "But you've got to tell us what you know."

The voice came through again. She sounded only about Katie's age, nine or ten, no older. She started talking about a circus and a caravan.

"It was just stood there by a Formica table," she said. "It had a dog collar on with spikes on it. I thought it was a dog at first, but it wasn't."

The presenter tried to encourage her. "You saw a dog in a caravan?"

"No. It was a pony." The voice was quite emphatic.

Sarah took over, leaning forward over the mike, eyes narrowed with concern: we were all gripped by what the girl was saying. "How big was it?" Sarah asked. "Can you tell us that?"

"It was a midget." The voice disappeared.

"Don't hang up!" Sarah almost yelled. She couldn't help herself. My heart was hammering. "Are you still there?"

"It must have something wrong with it." The words came out fast and jumbled. "It was so tiny – but it neighed, it definitely made a noise, because my dog started barking and that's when two men nearby noticed me looking through the window and I ran away."

It was bizarre. But it sounded genuine.

"Where was this?" Sarah asked. "Did you say a circus?"

The girl didn't answer.

"Are you still there? Hello?"

"We really need to know where," Ross tried, desperate for more information. But it was too late. The phone line clicked dead . . .

She'd hung up.

Chapter Three

"It's got to be a Falabella!" Ross screeched as we ran full pelt down the corridor, past reception and out through the revolving door.

Falabellas are the smallest breed of pony in the world and they are being bred more and more in this country. They originally came from Argentina and are so small they could actually sit on a person's knee.

"Are there any circuses in the area?" Sarah asked, fishing the car keys out of her handbag. "Come on, we've got no time to lose!"

"I think there's one on the common on the other side of town," said Blake.

The car groaned into gear, sounding as if something had died in the engine. Sarah slammed down the accelerator and nearly pulled out straight into a milk float.

"This can't be happening!" she groaned when she looked through the rear-view mirror.

We all turned round and stared out of the back window to see one of the *Breakfast Bunch* cars heading down the road towards us. Dominic was driving and Cassandra was hanging out of the window, trying to wave us down.

"They must have heard the radio show," I said bleakly.

But Sarah was giving them no chance to catch up. She shot off down the road with black smoke billowing out of the exhaust and all the pedestrians staring at us. There was non-stop tooting coming from behind and I didn't need two guesses as to who was blasting their horn.

"We've got to lose them," Sarah shouted. "If we don't, they'll ruin everything."

She shot up a side street, then realized it was a one-way system and had to back into someone's drive where she knocked over a plastic gnome.

"Let's get out of here!" Ross yelled, and then we saw the *Breakfast Bunch* car sail past on the main road. We'd lost them – at least for now.

"Come on, hurry up!"

We reached the circus ground fifteen minutes later, totally at a loss as to what to do next and pulled in behind a row of lorries where nobody was about. The big top was on the other side of the site and the caravans were sprawled all over the place. We'd just have to try and have a quiet snoop around. Sarah locked up the car and we slowly edged our way to the first caravan which was

18

brightly painted in yellow and red with some rather flamboyant costumes hanging on a washing line outside. Everything looked down-beat with a distinct air of poverty. Blake said people didn't come to circuses so much because of the cruelty aspect and also because they were outdated. This was the result.

We saw someone in the distance leading two ponies towards the big top and we quickly dived out of sight but they didn't see us. It appeared that everybody must be in the big top for rehearsals or maybe an afternoon performance – certainly outside it was pretty desolate. We looked through the windows of three more caravans but saw nothing.

"Wait! Let's think for a minute," Ross said, stopping dead in his tracks. "The girl said she was walking her dog – obviously here on the common. So it must have run off and the chances are it would have headed for the first caravan it came across which would mean one on the outskirts."

"Over there!" I pointed excitedly. There was a single caravan parked by itself some distance away from the others. All the curtains were drawn and it was hitched up to a rusty old truck with an open back.

"This must be it!" Sarah breathed.

"What's going on here?" Somebody dressed as

a clown but with a really deep, serious voice was standing directly behind us. And he wasn't smiling!

Sarah tried to explain. "We were just looking for our dog. It's slipped its lead. Have you seen a stray dog?"

It might have worked, it just might, if a familiar car with big letters down each side hadn't bounced on to the field at full speed with a cameraman fighting to get out of the door as soon as it stopped, and Cassandra tripping up over an array of wires which sent her sprawling on her hands and face.

"What's this, the Anneka Rice show?" The clown looked horrified. Our cover was blown.

He immediately shouted for someone called Jed, who was the circus manager, and immediately a big strapping man with an ear-ring in one ear came striding round the corner.

The cameraman was zooming in, filming everything, and Dominic just kept repeating, "Keep it rolling, keep it rolling."

The manager looked very angry.

"There's a very simple explanation," Cassandra babbled, backing off at the speed of light. "It's just a school project, that's . . ."

"Are you going to get off this land, or am I going to have to throw you off?"

He didn't mince his words.

"We've had it on good authority that there's a

pony being kept in one of your caravans." Sarah decided to jump in head-first.

"I've got nothing to say to you, nothing, do you hear me? Now clear off before I fetch the police."

"I think it's us who should be calling the police, don't you?" Sarah wouldn't give up.

"I don't know who you are, and quite frankly I don't care, just get out and take these raving ninnies with you!"

Dominic was hopping up and down with excitement, totally unaware of how heated everything was becoming.

"I'm warning you," the manager threatened, putting his hand over the camera lens and raising his fist to Dominic.

If we didn't get out of here soon, someone was going to get hurt.

The clown looked particularly menacing and even Sarah was backing off. The only way we could take a look round the circus was with a police warrant and we didn't have one.

The clown moved in on Dominic. "Listen, I don't care if you're the next Terry Wogan. Just leg it, OK?"

Dominic's face went as sickly green as his bow tie. Cassandra grabbed hold of his arm and dragged him back towards the car. I suddenly realized that Blake was missing. Where was he? He'd disappeared!

"Stay right where you are," the circus manager yelled. Blake was sneaking towards the caravan standing by itself, and he'd very nearly reached it. Just a few minutes more and he'd have been there.

"Do you want me to sort him out, Jed?" The clown looked as if he was itching for a good fight. It gave me the creeps to see someone dressed up as a children's entertainer behaving more like a gangster.

Blake turned round and walked slowly back.

"I don't believe it! It's Blake Kildaire!"

Sarah, Ross and I were knocked sideways. How did this Jed character know Blake?

"So it is," the clown gasped, holding out his hand and slapping Blake on the shoulder with the other. "How are you, mate?"

Obviously in all the chaos beforehand, Blake had kept a low profile.

"How did you get mixed up with a bunch of idiots like these?" Jed eyed us with a look of contempt.

"But how do you know Blake?" Ross couldn't resist asking.

"Didn't you know?" Jed cocked up his chin,

putting an arm round Blake and ruffling his dark hair. "He used to work here!"

"Well, you could have told us," I barked at Blake as we drove home to Hollywell.

"There was hardly much time, was there?" Blake said. "And besides, I didn't know it was going to be Jed's circus. I only worked there for six months and that was a couple of years ago. I needed the cash."

"You're such a dark horse, Blake, I don't think we'll ever know the real you." Sarah pulled into the Hollywell drive and we all tumbled out in a heap.

We'd known Blake for quite some time now and even though he'd lived with us on and off and helped us through the worst times of our lives, there was a dark mysterious side to him which always took us by surprise. Ross said it was because he was a Scorpio but Sarah described him as a natural introvert. Blake believed what lay in the past didn't matter, it was the present and the future which counted and that's what he was most concerned with.

He sat down in the kitchen with a cup of tea, his dark eyebrows knotted into deep furrows. "I don't agree with you, Mel – not all circuses are bad."

I couldn't stand the idea of any animal being caged up and made to do tricks and I wouldn't listen to any argument to the contrary.

"It's a way of life to them," Blake insisted. "All those animals are well looked after – there's no cruelty, at least not in Jed's circus. I can promise you that."

"So why did you go along with us to the circus?" I protested. "Why didn't you say something in the car?"

"Because—"

"Look, this isn't getting us anywhere," Ross interrupted. "We're no nearer to finding the Falabella."

"That's if it is a Falabella," Sarah said.

"It says here," Katie read from a book, "that Falabellas descend from the Shetland pony and the English Thoroughbred and they are only the size of a milk bottle when they're first born. Maybe it's a foal?"

"It sounds possible," Ross added.

"The main question is, where is it?"

"Mel's right," Blake said. "And we're running out of time. It won't be long before whoever's to blame hears about the radio show or our visit to the circus. We can't hang about."

"I agree," Sarah said, reaching for the phone. "I think it's time we called the RSPCA, don't you?"

Of course we'd been in this situation a million times before. By the time the RSPCA officer inspected the premises, any evidence of a neglected pony had completely disappeared. The circus now had good warning – if it hadn't been for *The Breakfast Bunch* tailing us we'd have been able to have a good snoop around and most likely find the Falabella. There was something very dodgy about that caravan; it was the only one which had all the curtains drawn in broad daylight.

Dominic and Cassandra sheepishly made an appearance a few hours later and didn't need reminding of how they'd messed up our operation.

"This isn't some kind of game, you know." Sarah was furious with them. "Thanks to you we'll probably never find this pony."

We were all grateful for the immense publicity *The Breakfast Bunch* would be giving us, but all they seemed interested in was a good story. They didn't appear to have any idea of what we were trying to do here – all they wanted was to score points with their bosses.

"It's not sensationalism. This is real life," Sarah finished. "Saving lives happens to be our job and we take it very seriously."

Cassandra was sipping some herbal tea nervously – she'd brought her own teabags – and Dominic was fiddling relentlessly with his bow tie. Ross had joked earlier that he must have had it made specially for him because it was so gaudy.

The atmosphere was tense, to say the least.

"I don't think you quite realize the exposure we will be giving you," Cassandra chirped up. "Have you any idea how much this filming is costing? And we were under the impression that Rocky would be here to star in it himself – where is he?"

Good question: plodding around somewhere in the Lake District was all we knew, and we couldn't admit that to *The Breakfast Bunch*. It was a fine time for Rocky to take a holiday – earlier that afternoon, before our own broadcast, we'd had Radio One on the phone, an early morning chat show and one of the teenage magazines, all wanting to talk to Rocky.

At one point Sarah had been so stuck for an excuse she'd said he was in the bath and couldn't be disturbed. News had leaked out that Rocky was staying at Hollywell and we'd had adoring fans hanging round the main gate gawping in at us ever since. Blake had tried to persuade them to go home but they wouldn't listen. Instead they asked him for his own autograph and Blake had nearly died of embarrassment.

Dominic came to the rescue in the end, deliberately making up a story that Rocky was at present in the local supermarket wearing a bright red wig and dark glasses. If they hurried they might just catch him at the check-out counter. It was cruel and a complete lie but it worked and for that we were grateful.

Blake was seriously worried about Colorado who was now a valuable show-jumper and it was essential to keep him safe and secure. With all these people around that was nearly impossible. The beautiful skewbald Mustang loved every minute of it and was delighted to be back with his old friends, Queenie, Sophie and Dancer. But I could understand why Blake was so concerned. Colorado meant the world to him – they were like one person.

It was now quite late at night. Katie and Danny had gone to bed insisting to Sarah that their latest brainwave was a stroke of genius – Hollywell Stables duvets and pillow cases and even special pyjamas. We had enough to cope with at the moment with the Hollywell Stables Fan Club. Since the release of *Chase the Dream* at the beginning of the week letters were pouring in by the sackload.

Dominic and Cassandra and the rest of *The Breakfast Bunch* crew were about to leave for their hotel, Cassandra insisting that Dominic was one of the best producers in the world. Dom, as he insisted we call him, had spent most of the evening telling us about his five children and his wife who was permanently at the hairdresser's and didn't understand him.

They were just about to get in the car when Rocky's stretch limousine swished up the drive and purred to a halt at our feet. Rocky leapt out, looking as bright as a button and gleaming with excitement.

"How's that for non-stop driving then?" he said, looking incredibly pleased with himself.

The sides of the limousine started moving at that point and we were all beginning to look nervous.

"Rocky, what have you got in the car?" Sarah shot backwards when we heard something grunt.

Rocky flashed us a wall-to-wall grin and flung open one of the limousine doors.

A huge hairy creature glowered out at us with tiny beady black eyes and great wads of rolling flesh. Its feet dug into the pristine leather seats and the smell was overpowering. It gave a huge grunt, tried to squeeze its way through the door and immediately got stuck. Rocky patted its head with affection and nearly got his fingers snaffled off for his trouble.

Cassandra gave a girlish scream and Blake burst out laughing.

"What on earth . . .?" Sarah was lost for words.

We all knew Rocky was capable of anything – but a pig in the back of his limousine?

"Meet my new partner," Rocky laughed, pointing to the pig which must have been the ugliest thing I'd ever seen. "This is Isabella!"

Chapter Four

"But it's a Vietnamese pot-bellied pig!" Ross croaked, as stuck for words as the rest of us.

"I don't believe this is happening," Sarah mumbled. "Rocky, how could you do this to us? Where did she come from?"

Dom and Cassandra stared in amazement. Rocky tried to coax Isabella out of the door but it was no use, she wouldn't budge. One of the cameramen suggested putting it all on film and Sarah practically howled with embarrassment. We'd lost a Falabella and gained a pot-bellied pig – what kind of horse and pony sanctuary were we?

"I didn't have any choice," Rocky explained. "It was bring her here or leave her for the chop – she'd have ended up as sausages if I hadn't saved her life."

"She looks distinctly like my mother-in-law," Dom observed, moving in for a closer look.

Cassandra stifled a giggle and slumped against the side of the limousine. "She's the strangest-looking pony I've ever seen."

Sarah went bright red and I started to see the funny side. Blake winked at me and Rocky said she was very sweet once you'd got to know her and he should know because he'd travelled all the way from the Lake District with her on the back seat. Ross collapsed into peals of laughter and none of us could keep a straight face from then on, especially when Rocky described his visit to the drive-in burger bar and how Isabella had scoffed half a dozen cheeseburgers and the attendant had thought she was a pet orang-utan.

"I'm surprised you weren't arrested," Cassandra commented, and Rocky explained how he'd then been recognized and had to give everyone his autograph, including the head chef and the toilet attendant. From that moment everyone at the burger bar was more taken up with *Chase the Dream* than Isabella.

"I think she's utterly marvellous," Cassandra cawed.

"Watch out!" Rocky yelled, just in time as Isabella squealed like crazy and flew back inside the limo, banging her head on the sun roof and spilling out of the opposite door, which Blake was holding open.

"She's out!" he yelled, lunging at her neck and missing completely.

"Don't let her run off!" Rocky shouted, grasping for her tail and clutching at thin air.

Dominic brandished his spotted umbrella, which he'd grabbed from the car seat, and Isabella went scuttling straight for Cassandra's legs.

"Stop her!" Cassandra screamed, fighting to pull down her skirt.

But there was no time. Isabella bulldozed straight between her legs and charged off across the stable yard, her huge belly lolling against the cobbles.

"Catch her!" Rocky shouted, not a bit concerned for Cassandra, who was screeching at the top of her voice and calling Isabella all the names under the sun.

"Love is so fickle," Dom philosophized, and then went and sat in the *Breakfast Bunch* car, out of harm's way.

Sarah escorted Cassandra back to the house, where she cried buckets, and I ran down the drive to close the five-barred gate, at least to prevent Isabella running on to the road.

"Got her!" I heard Rocky shout and when I arrived back in the yard, he was being dragged along on his boot heels, desperately trying to hang on to a fat and hairy hind leg, which was darting out in all directions.

"Ouch!" he howled as Isabella clouted him good

and proper on the kneecap. "Come back here, you great lump of lard!"

Ross and Blake jumped on her, one at each end, and I flung a leadrope round her neck just in the nick of time.

"Blimey, she's as strong as a pit pony," Rocky gasped, rubbing his knee and sticking his tongue out at Isabella, who was snorting in total disgust.

"Something tells me we're stuck with her," Ross commented in a tight voice. And I had exactly the same feeling.

"So you see now why I had to bring her home."

Rocky ripped open another packet of chocolate biscuits and tentatively examined the knee on his black leather trousers which had split open. Sarah was hunting under the sink for some TCP but the nearest thing she came to was some household bleach and Rocky nearly ran a mile.

Apparently Rocky had received a phone call from an "actress" friend of his called Rose. She called herself an actress but hadn't actually played in anything, apart from being a tree in a play at a fringe festival, and that didn't really count. She'd bought Isabella when she was just a few weeks old for a vast sum of money, simply because it was the latest craze among the rich and famous.

From the very beginning Isabella had been a rebel. She chewed up everything in sight and stacked on weight by the ton. She'd even become obsessed with watching television and, as a final resort, Rose had spent a fortune on a special pet psychiatrist but he only lasted two weeks, resigning on the grounds of mental stress.

Rose then seized the opportunity to travel the world with her new millionaire boyfriend and Isabella had been left unattended and completely forgotten. She'd ransacked the country mansion in the Lake District where Rose had been residing and escaped into the local village, demolishing the general store and causing two old ladies collecting their pensions to have funny turns. One of the farmers threatened to shoot her and put her in the freezer which was when Rose, alerted by a neighbour, contacted Rocky from Monte Carlo and demanded that he do something about the "Beastly Horror".

"The poor sweetheart," Sarah said; it was such a heart-rending story. "She's totally misunderstood."

"She's totally spoilt." Ross added.

Isabella was at present locked in one of the stables, digging up the straw bedding and scowling ferociously at Danny and Katie, who were running around outside in their pyjamas, having been woken by all the noise in the yard.

"We'll sort her out," Blake promised without the slightest doubt. "What's a mere pig compared to a wild Mustang?"

If anybody could do something with Isabella it was Blake. He had a special way with animals which was quite remarkable. They just seemed to do whatever he wanted. Colorado, who had become quite the local celebrity, wouldn't let anybody on his back apart from Blake and maybe me if Blake was close by. Sarah said he had special powers but I think it was because he was so gentle. He never lost his patience, no matter what, and I was convinced that was his secret.

The next morning Dom and Cassandra were on the scene, bright-eyed and bushy-tailed, determined to do some good filming. Cassandra was ecstatic because Rocky was still at Hollywell although he had a TV show to do that afternoon for Channel Four. She followed him around like a love-sick puppy, reeking of perfume and wearing a black and white checked headband which showed off her snow-white forehead and made her look as if she'd just come off the tennis courts. As Rocky wasn't the sporty type I couldn't see the point of it all, but apparently she had been grilling Katie and Danny for information on Rocky's likes and dislikes and they thought it a real hoot to feed her false information. By lunchtime she was spouting on about politics and Rocky looked bored out of his brain and was making every excuse he could think of to get out of her clutches.

The filming started off badly. Boris, who had just recovered from a snapped tendon and was being let out of his stable for the first time in weeks, refused to pose for the camera. Within the first few minutes he had stood on my toe and then carted me off down the field, splattering mud in my face and refusing to be caught. Queenie, our lucky mascot, equally camera-shy, just stood staring into the lens with a peculiar blank expression and wouldn't move an inch. Jigsaw continued to prove he was star material by rolling in front of the cameraman and waving all his paws in the air.

In the end Rocky took over, which didn't please Dominic in the least and he went and sat in the kitchen and drank gallons of Cassandra's herbal tea, which smelled and tasted like boiled spinach.

We finally heard from the RSPCA. It was as we expected – they hadn't found anything suspicious. There was no sign of any pony in any of the caravans at the circus. All the animals were in excellent condition and it looked very much as if we were barking up the wrong tree. *The Breakfast Bunch* crew were shattered with disappointment and that just made me more angry. All they wanted was a rescue case on film to bump up their viewing figures – it made me sick.

For months now, though, we had worked closely with the RSPCA officers and they had contacted us on numerous occasions with ponies desperate for a good home. People were beginning to sit up and take us seriously and Sarah said the RSPCA had every intention of keeping their eyes peeled and following up any potential leads.

"So what now? We're not going to just sit back and kick up our heels." Sarah was one of the strongest people I knew. Once she made up her mind to do something there was no stopping her. "There's a pony somewhere in trouble. I just know it."

Blake walked in wearing his suede chaps, which we'd bought him for Christmas. He had to keep schooling Colorado and his other horses in preparation for the competition season. But at the moment he was as concerned as us about the mystery Falabella.

"What if she's got it wrong? What if it wasn't a circus at all?" Ross was really using his head. "What if it was something that just looked like a circus?"

"Heck, you could be right." Rocky flounced into the room carrying his silver stage suit which he was going to wear for the chart show, *Top Hits*.

Rocky hated staying in hotel suites and whenever he was in England he crashed with us. He loved just being "normal" and had adopted us as his second family. The only thing Sarah drew the line at was his vacuum-cleaning – he was hopeless at it.

"So what else could it be?" Sarah tapped her head with her fist, desperate for ideas.

"A caravan site?" I suggested.

"No, no, something more obvious," Ross replied. "Come on, everybody, think!"

"I've got it!" Blake's face lit up. "It can only be one thing. The fairground – the local fair!"

"Or gypsies!" Ross added.

"Listen, wait, I've had an idea!" I didn't know why I hadn't thought of it earlier. "Roddy Fitzgerald! He'll know everything that's going on in the area. If anyone can help us he can!"

Roddy was a junior reporter on the *Weekly Herald*. He might not have been an ace journalist as yet but when it came to local knowledge he was a walking encyclopedia.

"Mel, that's it, you've got it!" Sarah raced off to use the phone.

At this point there was a howl of fury from Rocky, who had, up till now, been reclining on the sofa, peacefully watching the lunchtime news.

"What is it? What's the matter?"

Rocky looked horrified.

Ross grabbed the remote control and pressed frantically at the volume. Rocky collapsed on a footstool, his eyes glued to the screen.

"What is going on?" I demanded.

A flash of spiky blonde hair leapt from the TV screen and I was left in no doubt as to who it was.

Pandora Paris. She was a famous pop star from America who'd had a string of Number One hits and was just announcing the unexpected release of a new single.

Rocky howled, "She's done this on purpose. It's a deliberate ploy to knock *Chase the Dream* off the top."

Nicknamed Polka Dot Pandora because of her gaudy spotted outfits, Pandora Paris was an arch rival of Rocky. Instead of competing for the Number One spots like a good sport, she literally went for the jugular. She slated Rocky in public whenever she could, calling him all sorts of names including an "old has-been" with a "voice like a strangled canary". Rocky never retaliated but we all knew it hurt him deeply, and it was so unprofessional.

"What a slime bag!" Cassandra grimaced, coming into the room and defending her hero to the hilt.

Pandora had recently appeared on *The Break-*

fast Bunch and according to Cassandra had proved such a pain in the neck that they never wanted her back on the set. She was only twenty-one years old but acted like the ultimate prima donna.

"How did they keep this so quiet?" Rocky gasped, awe-struck that his manager hadn't breathed a word about it.

Pandora boasted that she was going to knock Rocky right out of the Top Ten; her single, *Snowflake*, was going to sell over a million copies and part of the proceeds would go to charity.

"The devious cow! She's trying to upstage us!" Rocky was furious.

The camera zoomed in on Pandora singing, and then went back to the news desk for a story on the Middle East.

"This is not good," Rocky breathed. "I think we can wave goodbye to the Number One spot."

"We're not going to let a jumped-up little upstart like that get the better of us," Cassandra spat out, surprising us all with her tenacity. "What is it you always say, Rocky? It's not over until the fat lady sings?"

"You're right . . . If Poison Pandora wants a fight then she's got one." Rocky leapt up, looking as if he could take on the equivalent of the Roman army. "She's not going to know what's hit her!"

Sarah came back into the room, getting the gist

of what was going on, but with other things on her mind. "I've just been speaking to Roddy," she said.

We all shut up and listened.

"There's a fair in town all right, a new one, over by the old estate."

"And?" Ross ventured.

"They've already been in trouble with the police."

Sarah hesitated and then went on, "They've got ponies!"

Chapter Five

It wasn't a proper fair. There was someone telling fortunes and another person giving pony rides. There were stalls set up selling crafts and household goods being sold from car boots.

A few caravans were dotted about and a couple of heavy draft horses were tethered on a patch of grass. Sarah wondered if the people might be Romany gypsies and Blake said they were just "travellers" and we shouldn't turn our noses up at them just because they were different from us.

All I was interested in was how they cared for their horses.

"Look, over there." Ross pointed to where a tubby black Shetland was tied to the back of a caravan with a foal laid down on the bare ground beside it. On second thoughts, it wasn't a foal but a yearling, and it didn't look as if it had ever been weaned.

"No, I can't believe that's what she saw." Sarah was referring to the girl on the radio. "We're looking for something smaller, much smaller, and what did she say about a dog collar?"

"Never mind the Falabella – what's this?" Blake was looking back towards the gate we had just driven through.

I caught my breath and had to look twice just to be extra sure. A hairy piebald pony about fourteen hands was trudging over the rutted ground with its head practically between its knees. But it was what it was pulling that made me wince in horror.

It was harnessed to a huge dray cart, loaded sky high with every kind of rubbish imaginable. Anybody with half a brain could see it was far too heavy for the pony.

"Stop!" Sarah yelled, running forward just as the piebald's knees started to buckle. One of the wheels had got stuck in a rut and it was impossible to shift the cart. An old man jumped down and started yanking the pony forward, slapping him on the flanks, jabbing him in the mouth, anything to get him to move forward.

There was someone else, probably the old man's son, who took over the reins and cracked them down on the pony's back. "Come on, yer stupid nag – move it!"

But it was no good. The piebald made one huge last effort, scrabbled for a foothold and went crashing down on his knees. It was horrible. He never even tried to get back up. The cart lurched dangerously and the two men slapped and battered his quarters, furious that he wouldn't get to his feet.

"Stop it. Stop it this minute!" Sarah looked manic. Her red hair had flown loose around her face and she was glowering.

She started pushing the men away and for a minute they didn't know what had hit them. Blake was already trying to undo the traces – the straps of leather which attached the harness to the cart. I was frantically looking for other straps to undo, as well as reassuring the pony in case he started to panic. He didn't seem to have enough strength in his front legs to heave himself up. I was terrified that he'd go crazy and start rearing and bucking. I'd heard of horses breaking their legs like sticks when that happened. But this pony seemed to be resigned to his fate. He didn't seem bothered if we got him up or not.

"You make me sick!" Sarah screamed, fighting to grab the reins from the older man who couldn't understand what all the fuss was about.

"He's just stumbled, that's all, he's always doing it. You'd think he'd know to lift his legs up by now."

"You stupid old fool," Sarah shouted. "Can't you see he's in pain. He can hardly walk!"

Ross had to try to calm her down because a minute longer and I think she would have hit both the men. I gently pulled the pony's forelock out of his eyes, which were gooed up and looked sore. He stared at me and then staggered and fell down again. "Blake, quick – help me!"

"Nearly there, old fella, just hang on in there!"

"Blake, hurry, he's bleeding!"

I couldn't believe the state of the pony's knees. They were so scarred and swollen, and now blood was oozing out, dripping on to the hard ground and staining the pony's legs red.

"Come on, Jakey, stop messing around and get up!" The old man was talking as if this was a game the pony played to get attention.

"Jakey, is that his name? Come on, boy, you're free now, up you get."

Blake, Ross and myself stood on either side of him.

"The poor thing's had it, Mel. If we don't get him away from here, he's going to die." I knew Blake was speaking the truth.

"Come on, Jakey, one big effort, that's all we need."

Slowly, ever so shakily, the pony lurched upwards. His whole body was trembling and patches of sweat had broken out underneath the huge filthy collar which pressed down on his neck. I wanted to scream out in anger that these two men had done this to an innocent pony. And they didn't even realize what was happening. They had no idea that Jakey was fast approaching the end of his tether. What were they going to do, keep driving him on until he collapsed on the side of the road?

Horses were treated like that in some countries abroad but here . . .? Blake put a hand on my shoulder and I realized tears were streaming down my face and a crowd of people had gathered round to watch and point and wonder. Yet again ignorance was at the root of it all – why did people own horses when they didn't have a clue about how to look after them?

Jakey seemed a lot happier now he was back on his feet. He was even nuzzling at my pockets where I'd got some horsenuts. Blake examined his knees which were cut to ribbons. The technical term was "broken knees", which came about when horses fell down and broke the skin, leaving scars. Often show horses and competition horses wear special knee pads to prevent this happening. But nobody had ever thought to put any on poor Jakey.

"He's well into his twenties," Blake said, examining Jakey's teeth which were blackened and sloping badly at the front. Blake suspected he may have had arthritis in his knees which would explain

46

the stiffness but we needed James, our vet, here to be extra sure.

"There's no way I'm paying for vet bills." The old man was adamant.

"Listen, Mister, this pony needs medical care." Sarah was trying to keep a lid on her temper, which was hovering at boiling point.

"It's Mr *Richardson*, and as for the pony, you can forget it. He's never needed no vet before. Wash his legs down with an 'osepipe, he'll be as right as rain."

"You're wrong, Mr Richardson. I've got a good mind to set the hosepipe on—"

"OK, let's get his legs cleaned up," Blake interrupted, taking charge. "And then we'll decide what to do."

"Five hundred pounds?"

"It's a generous offer for a pony that's never going to work again." Sarah was offering to buy Jakey from the Richardsons and retire him to Hollywell Stables. We kept a special fund of money for this very purpose.

"Take it, Dad. We could buy a van with the dough."

"Why don't you make it a thousand?" Mr Richardson was not going to make it easy.

"Because we can't afford that much," Sarah barked. "He's not worth that much and you know it."

"He seems to be worth a lot to you." Mr Richardson rolled a cigarette and examined his fingernails.

"Look, we can make it hard on you," Sarah fought back. "All I have to do is call the RSPCA. There are enough witnesses here to back me up."

"Do you really think anyone will take your side?"

"There must be someone here who saw what happened."

"The pony slipped. He's feeling under the weather. We're going to retire him. End of story." Mr Richardson put the cigarette in his mouth and reached for some matches.

"So you are going to retire him?"

"I said I would, didn't I?"

"Yes, but why is it that I don't believe you?"

"Listen, Miss Goody Two-Shoes, you've done your Florence Nightingale bit, now buzz off and leave us in peace."

Mr Richardson stomped off to his caravan and slammed the door shut behind him.

"I'm bringing a vet back with me!" Sarah yelled. But nobody answered.

*

"What? All this happened and we weren't there?" Cassandra and Dom were devastated that they'd missed the action. But the last thing we needed was the *Breakfast Bunch* car trailing after us like a bad smell. If it hadn't been for them we might have found the Falabella at the circus.

"So what are we going to do now?" All I could think of was poor Jakey tethered up behind a caravan looking desolate and so alone. He'd watched us all the way back to our car and it had been awful having to drive off and leave him.

Sarah was desperate to get in touch with James.

"I can't understand why he wouldn't sell him." Ross was as wound up as the rest of us. "Surely it would have been the best way out?"

"I can't believe there're still people using horses and carts." I'd heard of rag and bone men but I never imagined there were still some in operation.

"It's all about tradition," Blake tried to explain. "To Mr Richardson, getting a van instead of a horse and cart is selling out on his past. He's stuck in his ways."

"I know where I'd like to stick him," Sarah said, steam practically coming out of her ears.

"This might be your chance," Ross said, staring fixedly out of the window. "Look who's coming up the drive."

It wasn't Mr Richardson. It was his son.

"I'm not looking for trouble. I just want to talk."

He came into the kitchen, holding his flat cap in his hand and looking down at his feet. He'd biked all the way from the caravan site and Sarah was furious with Cassandra when she offered him a cup of herbal tea.

"I'll get Jakey to you by six o'clock tonight. But I want half the money up front." He didn't beat about the bush.

"How do we know you're not trying to rip us off?" Blake asked, suspiciously.

"You don't. But if you want to see Jakey again you'll have to trust me. As far as I can see, you've got no choice."

"Cocky little creep, aren't you?"

"Ross, leave it. We'll give him the money." Sarah had made up her mind. "I'll just fetch my cheque book."

"Er, no cheques, please. We don't have a bank. Me dad insists on cash on the nose."

It took ages to get two hundred and fifty pounds together. We only had a hundred and fifteen pounds, including mine and Katie's pocket money, so Dom and Cassandra emptied their pockets too, and Blake gave us the money he had won on Colorado at Olympia. We counted it all out, put it in a biscuit tin and handed it over.

"You better not let us down. If you do a runner—"

"I'll have him here at six on the dot. You'd better be waiting."

We prepared a stable, filled a haynet and put down a fresh straw bed.

Rocky had set off earlier to perform live on *Top Hits* so he had no idea what was going on. Dom and Cassandra insisted on hanging around to film Jakey arriving at Hollywell Stables. Katie, Danny and myself killed time by going through the sackloads of mail which we'd received in the last week. Most of it was from people wanting to join the Fan Club and requests for sweatshirts, mugs, pens and so on. Even so, it was a mammoth task and would take us more than just a few hours to sort out.

By ten to six we were all jumpy and Katie and Danny kept running to the bottom of the drive to see if there was any sign. Ross aired his views that they'd probably packed up and left town hours ago and Blake had to admit he felt the same way.

By half past six we were all filled with doom. We'd been taken for a ride and it had cost us two hundred and fifty pounds.

"The lying, rotten scoundrel," Sarah fumed when there was still no sign. "We should have known better. We've been taken for right mugs."

"But he seemed so genuine," I insisted, feeling forlorn. "Maybe he'll still turn up."

"And pigs might fly."

Of course we should have known better. Anybody who could neglect a pony couldn't be trusted and we'd walked straight into it. But it was so easy when you were desperate to believe only what you wanted to believe.

By half past seven the stable was still empty.

"Sarah, hurry up. You'll miss it!"

We gathered round the television set to watch Rocky and the first showing of the *Chase the Dream* video. Ross was frantically looking for a blank tape to put in the video and Katie was terrified he'd record over her tape of Olympia.

Pandora Paris came on with her song, *Snowflake*, and we all booed and hissed. Cassandra even went so far as to throw a cushion at the TV.

There were a couple of heavy metal bands and then the cameras zoomed in on Rocky who was up on stage with hordes of girls shrieking at him and artificial smoke billowing out of a special machine.

"What's happened to the video?" Sarah was so nervous she was chewing her nails.

Then we saw it on a big screen behind Rocky and the rest of his band. It looked fantastic.

"There's Queenie," Katie squealed. "And Boris!"

"Isn't that you?" I pointed to where someone was hovering around in the background with a sou'wester pulled over their eyes.

"It certainly is not," Sarah said, going red in the face.

Chase the Dream faded out and the presenter wound up the show by predicting a new Number One for next week. But who would it be, Rocky or Pandora?

"Oh, shut up," Ross growled at the presenter who'd been getting right up his nose.

Dom was in a mood because Jakey hadn't arrived. Sarah sarcastically remarked that he was more interested in the film than in Jakey. Cassandra tried to keep the peace and then before we could decide what to do next, Katie came running in from outside with more bad news.

"It's Isabella, she's gone! She's vanished!"

The stable door swung open and there was no sign of her in the yard.

"The pig has well and truly bolted." Dom stated the obvious.

"So what now?" Blake asked, and none of us had any idea.

"She's in the High Street!" Sarah exclaimed,

coming off the phone to the police. "Last seen heading for the pizza parlour!"

We didn't need any more prompting. We dived off in the *Breakfast Bunch* car, Sarah taking the wheel and not stopping to consider how we were all going to catch her.

Sarah was in such a stew that she took the wrong turning at the mini roundabout and had to do a U-turn in the middle of the road, holding up four cars.

"Excuse me, have you seen a pot-bellied pig?"

Four lads dressed up for a night out gazed through the lowered window at Sarah as if she was off her head.

We'd already been past the pizza parlour twice and there was no sign of Isabella but further down there was a police car parked outside a new super posh Indian restaurant which had just opened. We knew something was up when we saw the guests piling into the street and one of the chefs ranting and raving and throwing his arms in the air. I knew we had found Isabella.

It was even worse than we'd expected. She'd ransacked the main dining area, upsetting tray-loads of poppadoms, and when we caught up with her she was rolling enthusiastically in curry, which was embedded all over the carpet.

"Can you please get it out of here!" One solitary

woman stood on top of a tables trembling from head to toe, her skin tone matching the colour of her salmon-pink dress. "I think I'm going to faint!"

The police were not amused. Neither was the restaurant manager who harped on about insurance and how we weren't fit to look after animals.

Dom and Cassandra waited in the car looking po-faced and embarrassed. Since they had arrived at Hollywell we'd failed to find the Falabella, lost track of Jakey and let a pig escape into a public place. It was not the kind of image we were supposed to be portraying.

It took us ages to get Isabella home. Once she realized we were trying to catch her she hid under a table and tried to bite anyone who came near her. Blake eventually managed to throw a blanket over her head and six of us bundled her into the car before she had time to retaliate. It was a living nightmare.

We crawled into bed in the early hours of the morning with the sickening knowledge that everything was going wrong. It was Ross who heard the telephone ring at seven o'clock the next morning and stumbled downstairs to answer it.

As soon as I realized it was Mr Richardson's son I was down the stairs like a shot and hopping around barefoot on the cold tiles, straining to hear what was being said. I didn't have to try too hard. Mr Richardson's son spoke exceptionally loudly on the phone and I could hear everything crystal clear. What he said shot through me like an electric shock.

"It's Jakey – he's collapsed!"

Chapter Six

He was stranded at the bottom of a hill. It was one of the steepest hills in our area and he'd collapsed in a heap with no intention of getting up.

The police were on the scene because there was a tailback of cars in both directions. Nobody could get through. The overloaded cart had been unhitched and someone had pushed it on to the grass verge. Mr Richardson was arguing with the police officer and Jakey lay splayed out in the middle of the road with just his ears moving back and forth and his head rising up every now and then. A car tooted its horn but Jakey didn't flinch – he'd had enough. He'd finally given in. The look of defeat was etched all over his face. He just wanted to close his eyes and drift away.

"No!" Sarah's voice cut through the early morning air like a sharp knife.

A vet whom we didn't know had been called out and after examining Jakey concluded that he had a bad heart and he couldn't be saved. He was fishing around in the back of his car for the humane killer, a special pistol which puts a bolt through a horse's head and kills it instantly.

"I won't let you," Sarah warned, instinctively moving back and putting herself between Jakey and the vet.

"We've got to get him off the road." The police officer acted as if he just wanted the whole problem to go away. He rubbed his stomach, apparently more interested in getting his breakfast than helping Jakey. The vet loaded the humane killer.

"For God's sake, give him a chance." Sarah was getting desperate.

Blake took the initiative. Ross, Katie, Danny and myself followed suit. We plonked ourselves down in the middle of the road and refused to move until someone called James.

"If an old man collapsed in the street with heart trouble you wouldn't put him down," Sarah reasoned, trying to buy time.

"But we're talking about a pony, not a human being." The police officer warned us that we could all get arrested if we didn't move off the road. Some of the people waiting in the traffic jam had come across and were listening to the conversation.

We couldn't believe it when a woman in a straw hat who looked as if she was going to a wedding sat herself down on the hard tarmac beside us.

"Well, I think that makes my feelings clear," she said. "Anybody going to join me?"

"Yes!" Katie and Danny yelled, raising their fists in the air when an old age pensioner grasped hold of his walking stick and tottered over to join us. "Where there's life there's hope," he stated and stood over Jakey like a protective sentry.

The police officer was beginning to get worried. It was turning into a full-scale demonstration. More cars were piling up.

"Hang on in there, Jakey, we'll save you." I took off my coat and gently placed it under his head so he wasn't pressing against the hard road. I stroked his whiskery, wrinkly nose and watched the rise and fall of his ribcage. Time was fast running out.

"I can't stand around here all day," the vet protested. "I've got other calls to make."

"You don't have to," Sarah said. "I've just telephoned our vet on the car phone. He'll be here in a few minutes. We're a sanctuary, we know what we're doing."

"Hey, you!" The police officer spun round just as Mr Richardson, who'd been keeping a very low profile, was trying to slope off without anyone noticing. "Come back. I haven't charged you yet."

Mr Richardson was in trouble for driving a dangerous vehicle on the road and causing a public hazard. At least he wasn't getting off scot-free.

"I'd rather the old 'orse dies here and now than this bunch of do-gooders get him." Mr Richardson spat the words out with such venom it took us all aback.

"Leave it, Dad, I've taken their money. Jakey belongs to them."

Mr Richardson's son appeared from nowhere.

"I tried to tell you but you wouldn't listen."

Sarah went to fetch the horsebox. James arrived two minutes later.

"OK, boy, let's take a look at you." James moved his stethoscope over Jakey's chest and asked Mr Richardson questions which he refused to answer. Jakey laid his head back on my coat, gave a long sigh and half closed his eyes. The woman in the straw hat was so upset she had to turn away. "His heart's extremely weak. He's a very old pony. He's exhausted."

"What are you trying to say, James?" Ross was gritting his teeth to fight back the emotion.

"Let's get him to Hollywell. He might just make it."

James had always said that Hollywell Stables was a magic place because all our animals seemed to defy nature and fight back from the brink of death. But I think we all knew it would take every ounce of magic to save Jakey. None of us, however, was going to give up on him.

Sarah backed in the horsebox as everyone moved their cars on to the verge to let her through. Quite a few people had turned round and taken a detour through the next village. But the ones who stayed had got totally caught up in the drama. The pensioner with the walking stick, whose name was Bert, had laid his jacket over Jakey's quarters to keep him warm. One little girl had pressed into my hand a handful of grass which she'd picked for him. Everyone was willing Jakey on and it soon got around that we were from Hollywell Stables. Somebody asked where Rocky was and someone else left a car door open and *Chase the Dream* drifted out from the car radio. I'd never be able to listen to that song again without thinking of Jakey.

Getting him into the horsebox was a taxing experience. We'd finally had the ramp extended and a winch and sling fitted but it was still nearly impossible to move him. Finally everyone gave one last heave and we all breathed a sigh of relief. He was in.

"He will be all right, won't he?" Mr Richardson's son looked genuinely upset. Even more so when we couldn't tell him what he wanted to hear.

"Leave 'it, lad. It's just an 'orse. We'll soon get another one."

Blake looked as if he was about to throttle Mr Richardson.

"Over my dead body," Sarah hissed, burning up at the thought of Mr Richardson mistreating another innocent animal. "You've not heard the end of this, not by a long chalk."

"How could someone do this?" Rocky arrived back from Top Hits, completely shaken about Jakey.

He hadn't seen as many cruelty cases as we had, only Dancer, a racehorse who had pneumonia when we rescued her, and his own horse, Terence, so the sight of Jakey laid out in the fresh straw threw him completely. He had tears in his eyes when he stroked Jakey's black and white coat and felt the bones under his taut skin. The sores from the collar around his neck were so deep and matted that James suggested we leave them at least until tomorrow. "Let's wait and see if he survives the night." And with that the reality of the situation hit home. The next few hours were crucial.

We all agreed to take it in turns to sit up with him. It was something we did for all our rescue cases and it was the twenty-four-hour care and attention which often pulled them through. Rocky insisted on doing a shift even though he had three interviews lined up for the following morning. To Rocky, saving Jakey's life was far more important than appearing on television. But it was Rocky's career on the line and we didn't want that to suffer on our account.

"Besides," Sarah said, "*Chase the Dream* is for Hollywell Stables. The best way you can help Jakey is by getting it to Number One."

"And sticking it to Poison Pandora," Ross joked. It was the first time any of us had laughed for days.

Jakey survived the night. I took over from Blake at five o'clock in the morning and he was in such a deep sleep he never even noticed me go into the stable.

Blake looked shattered but insisted on staying with me for some extra company. We talked about everything from show-jumping to Colorado and what we both hoped for the future. We rattled on for hours and then at seven o'clock Rocky popped his head over the door, saying he hadn't been able to sleep a wink and did we realize it was Easter this coming weekend?

Rocky laid his hands on Jakey's chest and closed his eyes. Someone had once told him that he had healing hands and he said anything was worth a try. He had the most beautiful long artistic fingers and on each one was a ring in a different colour.

His long black hair drifted down over his shoulders and, still dressed in his silk pyjamas, he looked like a strange vision which had just appeared in front of Jakey.

Blake and I stayed very quiet and ten minutes later Jakey opened his eyes and tried to lift himself on to his shoulder. Whether it was coincidence or Rocky's special powers I suppose we'd never know. The main thing was he was still alive.

James could hardly believe the transformation. We all had breakfast together and then the TV crew turned up for the last day's filming. Rocky said they were trying to stretch it out so they could live it up on expenses at the local hotel.

They were mortified when James refused to let them anywhere near Jakey. He needed his rest, which meant no disturbance. Cassandra turned her attention to Isabella who was so furious because we'd put her on a diet that she was trying to chew her way through the stable door.

At least we'd won our spurs back as a sanctuary. We'd saved a horse and a pig and *The Breakfast Bunch* team seemed happy with their film of the other horses. The only thing we hadn't done was to track down the mystery Falabella.

"We can't let it drop," Blake said, raking his hand through his thick black hair. Even though Blake had his own life now as a show-jumper he was still intensely interested in the sanctuary. He was part of the Hollywell team and he always would be.

We didn't know for sure that there was a mystery foal or pony or whatever, but we had to exhaust all possibilities before we called it a day. There was no way we could go back on the radio, appealing to the young girl, because whoever had the Falabella might get wind of it and do a runner. Roddy Fitzgerald, our friendly reporter, had checked out other leads and come up with nothing. There was only one thing for it – we had to go back to the circus!

"I just can't imagine Jed being involved," Blake insisted, referring to the circus manager.

Blake had told us all about how he had been hired by Jed a couple of years ago to look after the eight white Arabian stallions which formed one of the best acts in the circus. There were also three shire horses and six Shetland ponies which were trained to race round the ring and pass underneath the shires. All the horses were stallions because they were the best performers and Blake had to be up at six every morning to wash the Arabians and prepare for the afternoon performance. If there was the slightest stable stain on any of the horses, Jed used to send him to muck out the camel, who was called George and used to spit at everyone.

Danny was so bowled over with Blake's stories that he was determined one day to join a circus. Sarah was not in the least bit enthusiastic because we were all in favour of animal-free circuses.

"It's not that simple," Blake said, cutting into her lecture about how bad circuses were. "It's never so black and white. There are some really good circuses and equally there are some really bad ones. It's like everything in life, you can't tar everything with the same brush. You've got to look at it individually."

"But even if the animal acts aren't actually cruel, what about all that travelling?" Sarah retaliated. "You know as well as I do they're dragged round week after week, cooped up on the back of lorries. You're not telling me that's a good life for a horse?"

"What about show-jumpers? Don't they spend most of their lives out on the open road? And believe me, they're under far more pressure than circus horses."

Sarah didn't have an answer.

"If you ask me," Blake went on, "it's far better to be looked after like a racehorse in a circus than to end up being sold for meat. And if you want the real truth, a lot of Jed's Shetlands have been saved from just such a fate."

*

James spent the rest of the day trying to keep Jakey as quiet as possible, which wasn't easy with Dancer neighing to him every five minutes and Isabella rooting in her stable and bulldozing at the door.

James gave us a special tonic to put in Jakey's feed which would help build him up, and was now talking about an electrocardiogram to examine his heart. Jakey's teeth were so long at the back they were cutting into his cheeks. No wonder the poor thing was thin – even if he'd had lots of food he wouldn't have been able to digest it properly. James fixed a huge metal clamp in his mouth to rasp his teeth and I had to hold his tongue to one side which was awful. All the time I kept thinking he might have a seizure. Jakey was gaining strength by the hour but James said he wasn't out of the woods yet.

Meanwhile, the telephone didn't stop ringing. Since *Top Hits* everybody suddenly wanted to know us. Ross was bowled over by the number of girls from school trying to angle for a date and I was overwhelmed when a researcher from *Blue Peter* rang up and wanted to speak to me personally. *Newsround* was on the phone wanting to do a special programme on horse care and the pony magazines were clamouring for exclusive pictures. It was slowly beginning to dawn on all of us that Hollywell Stables was becoming famous!

"Never mind fame," Rocky said, having just returned from yet another TV recording. "We've got a job to do."

"No, Rocky, there's no way you can be in this – it's too risky." Sarah was trying to put her foot down but it wasn't easy. "Rocky, are you listening to me?"

Rocky was looking in the mirror, fiddling with a blond wig which he used as a diguise together with dark glasses. The last time he'd worn a blond wig was at Olympia where he'd been taken for a famous show-jumper.

"Rocky!"

But before Sarah could say anything else Katie waltzed into the room carrying a huge box of what looked like paints and brushes.

"There's no point arguing," Rocky said in his most dominant voice. "I'm going with you and that's that. Now come on – it's time to get ready!"

Chapter Seven

We were going to the circus!

And thanks to Rocky's brainwave, we had the perfect disguise. Sarah painted our faces; Katie and Danny were mice, I was a cat and Ross a dog. It was a brilliant idea. Nobody would recognize us.

The main objective was to have a snoop around as soon as the evening performance got started. Everybody would be so busy with their acts that hopefully they wouldn't notice us. Blake had to stay at home because he was too recognizable, but Sarah wore a headscarf and dark glasses and Rocky sported his blond wig which was in serious danger of blowing off. If he were recognized as a famous rock star, not only would he probably be mobbed, but it would be plastered all over the daily newspapers.

"For heaven's sake, Rocky, hold on to that wig," Sarah growled.

"Danny's got more whiskers than me," Katie complained, and then spotted a giraffe which immediately shut her up.

We'd brought the two of them along so we looked more like a normal family having a day out at the circus. Usually when we went snooping Sarah insisted they stay behind because it was too dangerous and, heaven knows, we'd had some sticky moments in the past.

We headed towards the big top, dreading that we might see Jed or the clown with the anything but funny face. As it was, we did see two clowns but neither was the one we'd met before and they were chattering in a foreign language and didn't even notice us.

The big top was half full, mainly young children with their mums and dads or grandparents. We sat down in the hard seats and Katie ripped open a packet of Jelly Babies which went flying into the row in front, a red one landing in an old man's coat hood. How Katie could think about eating at a time like this I really didn't know. We all jumped when Jed's voice boomed out and he walked into the ring dressed in a tailcoat and top hat.

The elephant was the first on, followed by the acrobats and then the horses. The Arabian stallions were amazing and I couldn't believe the speed at which they galloped round or the way they could turn on a sixpence.

Katie was mesmerized by the Shetlands who scurried in with ribbons tied in their manes and tails and promptly laid down and rolled over to order.

"Mel, wake up, will you?" I was so busy wondering how they taught the shire horses to shake hands that I didn't notice Sarah tugging at my jacket and Rocky already waiting for us outside. It was time to do what we had come for.

"Quick, in here," Rocky whispered five minutes later when a group of men in fancy costumes were heading straight towards us.

We dived into a tent and immediately regretted it as we were hit by the most terrible smell.

"It's George the camel," Katie shrieked as a huge brown animal lumbered out of the shadows and made straight for Rocky.

"Let's get out of here!" hissed Rocky.

Our main aim was to find the caravan which we'd seen on our first visit and where we were all convinced the Falabella was hidden. Sarah thought it a good idea though to check out the horse tent along the way. The Arabians had finished their act and were back in the temporary wooden stabling which Blake had told us about. The two grooms were standing round the back of the tent sharing a cigarette and we managed to sneak in and out without them even suspecting.

But it was a waste of time because we found nothing.

In order to get to the caravan we had to pass behind a row of articulated lorries which were parked on the edge of the site.

"You realize it could be in any one of these?" Ross said, but we had to believe what the little girl had told us. A caravan. Under a Formica table. Wearing a dog collar.

"Hey, you!" A cold hand of fear gripped me like a clamp.

It was Jed.

"What do you think you're doing?"

Jed had crept up on us, as quiet as a cat, from behind one of the lorries and now he was bristling with suspicion.

"Don't I recognize you from somewhere?" He was looking pointedly at Rocky.

I kept my head down while Rocky spoke in a high-pitched voice and babbled on about a cousin of his who was staying in the caravan "over yonder".

As yet Jed hadn't sussed who we were. The last time, he'd been so taken up with *The Breakfast Bunch* crew and Blake that I don't think he'd paid much attention to us. But the longer we hung around the more chance there was that he'd catch on and I didn't want to be standing next to him when he did.

"So you know those couple of lazy louts, do

you?" Jed's face blackened over like a storm. "Couple of swindling layabouts, those two. Call themselves jugglers – they couldn't juggle a beach-ball between them."

Sarah gave me a quick glance and Rocky tried to find out more information. Apparently Jed had hired the two brothers who said they were jugglers and were prepared to work cheap. They had a scruffy caravan which they kept locked up at all times with the curtains drawn and they went ber-serk if anyone tried to go near it. Rocky asked if they still had a pony and Jed looked blank, although he did say that one of the grooms accused them of pinching a bucket of horsenuts.

My heart leapt and I knew we were on to some-thing. All the pieces were fitting together.

"We'll just go and say hello then," Rocky squeaked, desperate now to get away before our luck ran out.

"You'll have a job," Jed grunted, about to turn on his heel back to the big top and the second half of the show. "They kept wandering off and missing shows, so I fired them this morning. They've packed their bags and gone."

How could we be so unlucky? We stood and stared at the empty space where the rusty old cara-van had been. We had missed them by hours.

"They could be anywhere by now," Ross said,

rubbing at his eye make-up which didn't seem to matter any more.

"Give us fifty quid and I'll tell you where they've gone."

We wheeled round to see one of the clowns we'd seen earlier standing directly behind us. He said he'd been in one of the lorry cabs and overhead everything.

"How can we trust you?" Rocky asked, already reaching for his wallet. It seemed we were handing money over to just about everyone these days.

The clown grasped hold of the crisp fifty-pound note and shoved it down his sock.

"So where are they?" Rocky's voice was back to its deep husky self.

"Take the main road to London – you can't miss 'em."

"Is that it? That's what I've paid fifty pounds for?"

The clown shrugged his shoulders.

"Come on, let's go," Sarah said, dragging Rocky away before he lost his temper.

"Oh, and by the way," the clown shouted after us, grinning like an imp. "That *Chase the Dream*, it's a cracking record!"

"The rascal knew who we were all along," Sarah

fumed, as we drove back to Hollywell.

"I think we ought to do as he says," Ross spoke up.

Rocky wasn't so sure. "It sounds like a wild goose chase to me."

Since we had set up the sanctuary we'd received a number of hoax phone calls – people making up stories just for a joke. It was cruel and vindictive but it didn't stop them thinking it was funny. It was more than likely that the clown had no idea where the jugglers had gone, he just wanted to make an easy fifty pounds. That was the kind of attitude we were up against.

"Let's decide when we get home," Sarah said, putting her foot down hard on the accelerator. We had to get Rocky back to Hollywell to do a live telephone interview for Radio One in approximately ten minutes' time.

Chase the Dream cackled out over the car radio. Mark Goodier cut in to give Rocky an enormous plug and make a few wisecracks about Poison Pandora. It wouldn't be long now before we knew who was the new Number One. Apparently Ladbrokes were even taking bets and I knew who I'd lay my money on.

"What on earth . . .?"

We rounded the last corner to Hollywell and Sarah slammed the brakes on in shock.

There must have been twenty or thirty people hovering around the gate, trying to get up the drive, every age group from teenagers to grown women, and when they saw who was sitting in the front seat of our Volvo they went wild.

"I told you to keep that wig on," Sarah said, as they all came galloping towards us.

"It's him! It's him! I told you!" a statuesque lady in a green tent dress flung herself at the car window on Rocky's side. Within seconds we were completely surrounded. Sarah couldn't move backwards or forwards and they were hammering on the windows and yanking at the door handles as if they'd taken leave of their senses. It was terrifying.

"Welcome to the fame game," Rocky said in a subdued voice.

We all knew he had trouble with fans but this was ridiculous.

"Don't open the doors, no matter what," Sarah said, trying to inch the car forward. One young girl flung herself on the bonnet and others pressed forward chanting, "Rocky! Rocky! Rocky!"

We managed to crawl up the drive and I vaguely saw Dom and Cassandra coming towards us and then Blake and James fighting their way through carrying a horse blanket which they threw over Rocky and whisked him off to the house.

The telephone started ringing – probably Radio

One – and then Blake appeared back outside, pushing the women towards the gate. I don't know what he said to them but they left as quiet as lambs.

Ross dragged me out of the back seat and then Katie and Danny appeared, waving a twenty-pound note in the air and smirking from ear to ear. I hadn't even noticed them getting out of the car. They'd sold Rocky's wig to the woman in the green dress!

I bolted towards the stables to check that Jakey was all right and had to spend five minutes talking to Dancer who was trembling from head to toe. Katie turned on her Mickey Mouse transistor radio (she had a thing about Mickey Mouse) to listen to Rocky, and Ross leaned against Dancer's door with his eyes half closed.

"I didn't think we were going to get out of that car in one piece," he breathed, obviously still shaken.

Dancer pushed her rose-pink nose into my pocket and I pulled out a carrot and offered it to her.

"You know, I actually thought being famous was a doddle," Ross went on, patting Dancer's long slender neck and flicking her mane on to the right side. "When everybody was ringing us and making such a fuss, it was all so exciting. I even thought about becoming a singer myself. But you know what? That's no way to live; that's living your life in a goldfish bowl."

Rocky always said that he wished in some ways he wasn't quite so well known. Being rich and successful brought a whole new set of problems which nobody really understood.

"Rocky's certainly right about one thing," Ross said, wiping at the smudged paint on his face which had run down his cheek and into his hair. "Fame is definitely not all it's cracked up to be."

We fed all the horses and rugged them up for the night. Jakey had special infra-red lights in his stable to keep him extra warm. Both he and Dancer were having boiled barley and linseed to help put on weight but we'd all forgotten to take it off the cooker hours ago and it had burnt to a cinder. Rocky volunteered to buy us a special boiler but we promised to be more careful in future.

"So what are we waiting for then?" Ross was itching to get going.

We'd just made an executive decision and there was clearly no time to lose.

"Here, take them." Rocky pressed a set of keys into Sarah's hand and wouldn't take no for an answer.

They were the keys to his limousine.

"You'll need a fast car. Now don't argue."

Sarah had driven Rocky's limousine when he stayed for Christmas and very nearly caused chaos in the supermarket car-park. It was as long as three cars and needed as many parking spaces. At first Rocky had had a chauffeur but now he preferred to drive himself around because it helped him relax.

"OK, OK, now can we please get going?"

Rocky offered to stay behind and guard the stables – we always left a babysitter, or rather horsesitter, in charge just in case anything went wrong.

Blake was coming along for extra support and even Jigsaw wouldn't stop barking until he'd clambered on to the back seat of the limousine and stuck his head in Rocky's portable fridge. Sarah turned the key in the ignition and Ross checked that the mobile phone was working. Sarah said she had a good feeling about this and Blake picked up a road map of Britain, offering to navigate.

"No need," Sarah said, turning left out of our drive and very nearly taking the holly tree with her.

"We're going one route and that's south," I added, perched on the back seat and looking straight ahead. "The main road to London!"

Chapter Eight

The motorway was half empty but that didn't make our job any easier. We'd been driving for hours and we'd seen nothing. The only caravan we'd come across was brand new and towed by a Mercedes – certainly not the one we were looking for.

Sarah cut across into the slow lane behind some lorries, and Ross said what we were all thinking – we were wasting our time.

"Let's carry on until the next stop-off place, then call it a day," Sarah said between clenched teeth. "At least nobody can say we haven't done our best."

We were all feeling tired and ratty and I had a crick in my neck from sitting in a draught because Danny had insisted on playing with the electric windows. Ross felt carsick and Katie had stuffed herself with so many sweets that she just felt sick, full stop. Jigsaw was surprisingly well behaved until Danny opened a box of chocolates and then he started drooling over the leather upholstery.

Sarah said Rocky wouldn't be very pleased but then we noticed where Isabella had ripped a chunk out of the back seat and we didn't feel so guilty after that.

The road stretched on for miles ahead, lit by the overhead lights. The limousine purred forward and Sarah said it felt like flying Concorde.

Blake tried to keep us all entertained by doing a horsy quiz in Katie's pony magazine.

"True or false? A bald face is when the face is entirely white? A filly is a foal under four years old? The Falabella is the smallest breed of pony in the world?"

We all went quiet after that and I munched on a Mintoe and tried not to think of a little pony stuck in a caravan. It was too horrible to contemplate.

Sarah banned Danny and Katie from watching the portable TV because it was after nine o'clock, past the watershed. Ross put a duster over his head because he said it helped his carsickness if he couldn't see anything. Katie finished off another nougat bar and then turned very pale.

We passed a sign saying "London, 30 miles," and another sign which meant refreshments ahead.

"I want the toilet," Katie whined, sitting tightly cross-legged with her lips pressed together.

Sarah said it served her right for drinking too

much Coca-Cola. "OK, gang, let's call it a day."

We went into a transport café after filling up with petrol and using the toilets. Blake said he was starving, and ordered chips and sausage, which made Ross look even sicker. Katie pinched most of his chips and I pocketed all the sugar lumps to take back for the horses. Sarah nibbled a dried-up doughnut and commented on two men sitting in the corner packing away steak-and-kidney pie and two pieces of chocolate cake each. Talk about having potbellies – if they weren't careful they'd end up looking like Isabella. One had a tattoo of a snake on his arm and the other scowled at us as if he had radar ears and could hear what we'd been saying.

"Let's just be thankful that *Chase the Dream* has been a success," Sarah said, washing down some black coffee which she insisted kept her awake. "And we've rescued Jakey who, fingers crossed, looks as if he's going to pull through. We can't save every horse and pony out there – it's impossible."

We all knew what Sarah was saying was true but it didn't make us feel any better. If only that girl hadn't come on the radio, we wouldn't be chasing round the country looking for a pony that probably didn't even exist.

The two men in the corner stood up and went

out and disappeared towards the toilets which Sarah was pleased about because she said they looked a bad lot. Then she drained her coffee cup and said it was time we were making tracks. We'd ring Rocky on the car phone and tell him we were heading for home.

We went out of the exit door which led to a different part of the car-park and there we all stood, rooted to the spot with our mouths hanging open.

Parked up against some trees, hidden in the shadows, was the same caravan and open-backed van we had seen at the circus.

"This is incredible," Ross said, suddenly forgetting his carsickness and looking wide awake. "I can't believe our luck."

We sidled over to the caravan as quietly and as quickly as we could.

"There's nobody about," Blake hissed, immediately trying to peep in through the closed door which had a bit of netting strung up at the window. It was the grubbiest caravan I'd ever seen. It was a dirty cream colour and the curtains at the windows didn't look as if they'd been washed for years.

"It's disgusting," Katie said, the palms of her hands black with sooty grime where she'd been trying to clamber up to look inside.

"What can you see?" I whispered to Blake who

was the tallest of the lot of us and was still spying in through the door.

"Listen – what was that?" He held up his hand and we all fell quiet, straining our ears.

I couldn't hear anything.

Blake tried the door handle but it was locked shut. "What do we do now?"

"Sssssh!" Sarah heard it clearly.

There was a definite noise. Something scrabbling and then the faintest high-pitched whicker.

"It's the Falabella!" Katie squealed. "There's a pony in there!"

"What now?" Blake looked to Sarah as if for instructions. There was no special manual on what to do in these situations. We just had to work on impulse and instinct.

"You do nothing," a voice boomed out from behind us and I turned round to see the man with the snake tattoo. My stomach flipped over and Katie grabbed hold of my arm. The two men from the transport café were obviously the two jugglers from the circus. And they'd got us cornered.

"You don't frighten me," Sarah said, her voice quaking. "We know what you've got in there. You can't get away with it. We won't let you."

"Just get out of my way." The man with the tattoo pushed forward. "Push off before we turn

84

nasty. You don't know nothing because you've seen nothing. Now get lost."

He grabbed Sarah by the arm and pulled her away from the door. Blake and Ross immediately moved in but they looked minute at the side of the musclebound jugglers.

"If you're looking for a fight I warn you, we used to be professional wrestlers."

There was no way Blake and Ross could take on these two. They were built like gladiators.

"We're not looking for trouble," Sarah said. "We just don't like cruelty."

"I don't know what you're talking about. Now get out of my way."

The frantic scrabbling from inside the caravan was a clear indication that he did know what we were talking about.

"I'm not letting you drive off until you open that door," Blake threatened, planting his feet firmly apart and looking as immovable as a tree trunk.

Blake was a tough cookie when it came to dealing with thugs. He'd sorted out someone called Bazz who'd tried to terrorize us and upset the horses. But these men looked a different kettle of fish. They didn't seem in the least bit scared of Blake.

The man with the snake tattoo made the first

move. He took a definite step towards the van and Blake immediately barred his way.

For one crazy moment I thought they were going to give in and open the caravan door but then, as quick as lightning, one of them pulled out his fist, and crashed it into Blake's ribs.

It was horrible. I didn't know what to do. Blake doubled over, coughing and spluttering, looking as if he'd ruptured his insides. Ross tackled the other juggler who merely put out his hand, grasped Ross around the neck and slammed his head against the side of the caravan.

Sarah's self-control snapped. She leapt on the back of the thug tackling Ross and started bashing at his arm with her fist.

"Mel, get help!" she screamed, as the juggler roared with rage and shook her off. "Do something!"

I caught sight of two of the transport café staff standing outside the exit doors, watching with their jaws round their knees. "Call the police!" I yelled, racing up to them, desperately trying to get a reaction. They were watching the scene as if it were something out of a soap opera and not actually happening in real life. I felt like shaking them but there was no time.

I ran into the cafeteria and spotted two lorry drivers tackling bacon butties but they ignored my pleas and turned their backs. They didn't want to get involved.

I was desperate now. This was no joke. We could all end up being beaten to a pulp. My heart was hammering so hard that my chest burned.

"Katie!" I yelled. "Katie!"

I stumbled across the car-park to where my little sister was racing around trying to outmanœuvre both the jugglers. She was clutching hold of some car keys and dodging this way and that as if her life depended on it. She must have got hold of the keys to the van!

Blake was staggering around trying to get his bearings and Sarah tended to Ross who was holding his head and leaning against the caravan.

"Throw them away!" I yelled to Katie who very nearly got caught as she lost her balance. "Chuck them, quick!"

Katie stopped still long enough to hear what I was saying and hurled the keys high and long into a clump of bushes.

The jugglers went berserk. Without the keys they couldn't get away. They were just about to leg it into the darkness when a white estate car zoomed round the corner, screeching on its brakes and cutting off their escape.

Even in the bad light you'd have recognized that car a mile off. Dom was driving and Cassandra was hanging out of the window with what looked like the sound man bouncing around in the back. It was the *Breakfast Bunch* car and for once they were right on cue. I don't think I'd ever been more relieved or grateful.

What happened next became the subject of conversation for months afterwards. Cassandra leapt out of the car looking murderous and proceeded to floor both the jugglers. Temporarily dazzled by the bright headlights, they didn't expect to be given the karate chop by a scatty-looking woman who'd appeared from nowhere.

The sound man backed her up by hitting the juggler with the snake tattoo over the head with a tripod. Even Dom used his initiative and quickly tied their hands behind their backs with some TV cable.

It was miraculous. A police siren wailed into the car-park and two officers leapt out just seconds later. Obviously the women in the café had finally got round to dialling 999.

Sarah, Ross and Blake staggered across, looking pale and shaken, and the jugglers started arguing among themselves and blaming each other. Sarah explained to the police officers exactly what had happened. The jugglers clammed up and wouldn't even give their names, but as they were bundled into the back of the police car the one with the snake tattoo couldn't help lashing out with pure venom.

"It's a freak! We were going to drown it. And we would have done if you lot hadn't turned up!"

It took two passing sales reps and the fire brigade to get the Falabella out of the caravan. We couldn't find the keys, which meant we couldn't open the door, and the windows were impossible to prise open. We didn't want to smash the glass in case the Falabella got hurt so in the end the firemen cut a hole in the door and we got in that way.

In the meantime the girls from the café brought across cups of tea and hot doughnuts, Dom and Cassandra went home and Ross was sent off to get his head bandaged. I fetched Jigsaw from the limousine. He obviously thought we'd all deserted him and had set about chewing up most of the back seat. There were bits of sponge and expensive leather all over the place.

As the door of the caravan creaked open my heart was hovering in my mouth. I really had no idea what we might find . . .

It was pitch black inside and there was a stuffy, stale smell. One of the firemen switched on a torch and shone it into the darkness. Blake was squeezing my hand and Sarah was pacing back and forth outside – she couldn't bear to watch. Even the fireman seemed nervous.

"What was that?"

"What?" Blake took the torch and lit up a tatty, filth-ridden Formica table. There were two mugs balanced on top, a box of teabags and an empty milk bottle.

The fireman felt for a light switch on the inside wall but there wasn't one.

"Further down," I whispered. "Shine it on the floor." I could hear something breathing. The first thing we saw was a dog lead coiled round the table leg.

My whole body was quivering with nerves and I didn't know whether I could bear to look. I heard Blake breathing beside me and I knew he was thinking the same thoughts. What if . . .?

And then we saw it . . .

It was curled up under the table, huddled in the back like a little dog with huge wide eyes like Bambi. It had the tiniest nose and a miniature head and a little tuft of hair which stuck up and served as a mane. There was a dog collar fastened round its neck.

"Heavens, it's so small," the fireman whispered. "It's hard to believe it's still alive."

But it was. It shuffled and half whinnied as Blake moved in closer and I couldn't stop staring at its delicate almost pinkish hoofs, which scrabbled on the lino. It was laid on its side and it was petrified of human beings but Blake gave it time to get used to him. He coaxed and whispered to it and gently extended his hand until he was touching its neck. It flinched backwards and hit its head on one of the table legs and then Blake was bundling it up into his arms, holding it steady and carrying it out of the caravan.

Sarah was waiting, holding out a blanket, and everyone moved back to give the animal some space.

Dom took one look and quickly walked back to the car with his head held down. It was always the ones you least expected to be emotional who got really cut up.

"It's a foal," Blake said, moving his hand along its tiny rump and feeling a short stubby tail. "The poor thing can't be more than a year old."

It had a blotch of white spots on its quarters, which meant it was an Appaloosa. They were the most sought after of Falabellas and it was probably worth a small fortune.

"How did it fall into *their* hands?" Sarah was stunned.

"I only wish I knew," Blake answered, burying his head into its soft, dark coat.

The Falabella foal turned out to be a little colt

and within minutes of finding him we'd already christened him Fluffy. It seemed the perfect name and it suited him down to the ground. He wasn't quite as weak as we'd first thought and although he found it difficult to stand, this was mainly because he'd been cramped up for so long rather than because of lack of strength.

We found a stale loaf of bread and a tray of water under the table which had obviously kept him going. The main thing now was to get him back to Hollywell as fast as possible and call in James.

Blake gently carried him into the back of the limousine, where thankfully there was lots of room, and in the front Ross held on to Jigsaw, who thought Fluffy was another dog and didn't understand why he couldn't play with him.

Sarah tried to drive as fast and as smoothly as she could but it was still going to be a long trek home. After twenty miles or so, Fluffy dozed off to sleep in Blake's arms, his long, delicate eyelashes flickering as if he were dreaming.

We all noticed that his near hind leg had a nervous twitch and there was an ugly welt across his upper thigh. I didn't say anything to Danny and Katie but it looked as if he'd been hit with something, maybe a belt or the lead. We'd removed the dog collar which had been fastened too tightly and had bitten into the soft skin around his neck.

"I hope he's all right," Katie said in a small voice as Blake gently scratched his tiny withers. Blake said that young horses liked the top of their shoulders scratched because it reassured them and reminded them of their mothers. It was certainly working with Fluffy. I couldn't help wondering who his mother was, where he'd come from and who he'd belonged to.

"He was probably bred in this country," Blake said, shifting his legs slightly because he'd got pins and needles. "There are quite a few Falabella studs up and down the country. After that, who knows, he fell into the wrong hands, he might have been stolen, whatever. I can guarantee he's not had the happiest start in life."

Whenever people thought about cases of cruelty they always imagined the animals to be cheap and worthless but in reality they were anything but. Look at Isabella who had been left to fend for herself and Colorado, a beautiful, talented Mustang. Any animal was vulnerable to ill-treatment, no matter what its value, and Fluffy was yet another victim.

"He's the most beautiful thing I've ever seen," Katie murmured, and I had to turn away with a giant lump in my throat and my eyes prickling with tears. Why did life have to be so unfair?

It took ages to get home because firstly Sarah took the wrong turning off the motorway and couldn't get back on to it, and then we were spot-checked by the police, who were trying to catch drunk drivers and were very suspicious of the limousine and whether we owned it. It seemed such a far-fetched story that it belonged to a famous rock star and that we had just rescued the foal in the back from two jugglers. They looked at us as if we were mad and insisted on asking loads of questions.

It was well into the small hours of the morning when we crawled up the Hollywell drive, low on petrol and low in spirits. We were all exhausted from the night's escapade. Ross was complaining of a headache and Blake was already turning black and blue.

"I hope they lock them away for ever," Sarah said about the jugglers, but we all knew that wouldn't happen. Despite all our campaigning, people still got away with hardly any punishment at all for the most horrific offences concerning animals. One day though it would all change, I just knew it.

James was already waiting when we arrived home. He'd been up all night with a dog who'd had a road accident and needed emergency surgery and then he'd received our phone call and driven over to Hollywell. Rocky was also up waiting, anxious and drawn, and trying to drink cocoa which looked sludgy and half cold.

"Is he all right?" he said, flinging open the back door as soon as he saw the headlights. Dancer, Queenie and Boris stared out of their stable doors as Rocky helped Blake carry Fluffy inside. There was a new resident at Hollywell and I think they sensed it.

Inside, under the bright light, Fluffy did look painfully thin. You could play a tune on his ribs and his legs were like sticks. James took one look at the colour of his eyelids and said he was anae-mic. He took his temperature, listened to his breathing and felt his tiny body all over.

Fluffy lay there, relaxed and resigned, every now and then flickering his eyes upwards towards mine as if to say thank you, thanks for saving me.

James said there was good and bad news. Firstly he didn't have any serious health problems and although badly malnourished he was young enough to recover. The bad news was that he'd broken a nerve in his hind leg, which would always have a nervous twitch. "He's definitely been hit with something," James said. "The poor lad's taken some right beatings."

Sarah filled a hot-water bottle and placed it under his blanket and Ross and Katie cornered off an area of the kitchen with the clothes-horse. Katie had always wanted a horse in the house and now she'd got her wish. I just wished it was under happier circumstances.

"The main thing is though," James said, taking a sip at Rocky's cold cocoa, "he's going to be all right!"

Chapter Nine

The Breakfast Bunch crew left with a tearful fare-well. Even Dom, who was hardly a country person, seemed more than a touch upset. He still hadn't got over Jigsaw chewing up two of his favourite sweaters but he bought all the horses a packet of mints each and Jigsaw a new bone which he could have probably done with in the first place.

Cassandra still had a huge crush on Rocky and left him all the telephone numbers she could think of, including her mother's, just in case he wanted more in-depth coverage. She'd also become extremely attached to Isabella who seemed to be settling down and actually allowed Cassandra to stroke her back, especially the ripples of fat on her shoulders. She'd already lost weight, although Cassandra did sneak her a bag of chips and got caught red-handed by Blake who gave her a lecture on the dietary requirements of pot-bellied pigs.

"For heaven's sake, everybody," Sarah said. "We're going to be in your studio in no time at all."

The last time we were actually in London was for Olympia, and all the Christmas decorations had been up. Both Katie and I had agreed it was the most beautiful city in the world. It was hard to believe we were going back to appear on a national children's television programme and meet loads of famous people.

"We've got Get This! [whose first album had gone double platinum] in the studio *and* Harry Enfield," Cassandra commented with a glint in her eye.

Danny was crazy about Harry Enfield and Katie thought Pete Jones from Get This! was just the business.

Sarah gave all the crew free Hollywell Stables sweatshirts and mugs and Cassandra gave us a box of herbal teabags, which, Ross whispered in my ear, would go straight in the bin.

We were all ever so grateful to Cassandra for her role in catching the jugglers. Who'd have thought she was a black belt in karate? Cassandra said she'd taken up self-defence because she lived alone in a flat in London. She'd already shown Danny a few of the important moves and he kept diving on everybody unexpectedly, like the man in the *Pink Panther Show*.

Lucky for us that Dom and Cassandra had suspected we were up to something and decided to follow us up the motorway – otherwise we might have ended up as mincemeat.

Fluffy looked a lot better in the morning and his legs weren't half as stiff. He soon got used to us and it was quite clear from the beginning that he adored Blake.

Sarah found out that the two jugglers had picked up Fluffy cheap from a horse sale and had decided to try and teach him a few tricks. They didn't know anything about ponies and thought Fluffy was a freak. When he didn't learn tricks they had beaten him with a leather belt.

"At least he'll be safe for the rest of his life now," Katie said, twiddling with his forelock. "I wonder just how big he'll grow."

James had warned us that he wouldn't grow to his full size. At the moment he was no bigger than Jigsaw.

"All the best things come in small packages," Blake said, and I was genuinely pleased that I wasn't tall for my age.

That morning we had received an enormous sack of mail. Someone had even sent a quilted navy blue rug which we thought would be ideal for Jakey.

Loads of people wanted to come and visit and

Sarah thought it was high time we organized a gala open day for the summer. In the meantime Katie and Danny decided to write out cards giving the history of each horse and pony and how they were rescued. These could be stuck on the relevant stable doors, covered with plastic sheeting and would be of interest to the hordes of visitors we were now getting.

Sarah was still harping on about building a special gift shop but the most important thing was a new stable block, barn and thirty acres of land. Each horse or pony needed preferably two acres of grazing land to itself and the way the sanctuary was growing we needed all the land we could get hold of. Pembroke Estates was now up for sale and Sarah was itching to make Charles Stonehouse an offer. He used to be the huntmaster of the Burlington Hunt and it was from him that we'd saved Boris. He hated our sanctuary but he needed money desperately and we were the only buyers on the market. Sarah had gone off to see the bank manager and hopefully organize a loan on the strength of the royalty payments from *Chase the Dream*. With any luck the Pembroke land would soon be ours.

"I think we ought to have looseboxes," Ross said, hanging up an assortment of headcollars in the tackroom. We couldn't make up our minds between a breezeblock-built barn with interior stabling or a row of wooden looseboxes. Sarah was seriously considering trying to get a special deal with one of the manufacturers. "Think of all the publicity we could give them, and we could have a special sign up saying, 'donated by so and so'." Sarah was a dab hand at getting freebies. She'd once managed to get a baby food firm to sponsor our horse show and she'd since got free woodshavings all winter in return for mentioning the company's name on radio. James said she could sell snow to the Eskimos if she put her mind to it.

"How do you spell 'piebald'?" Katie asked, smudging the card she was writing with a red marker pen. She'd already put, "Jakey. Fourteen hands. Saved from a nasty man who worked him into the ground."

"You can't put that," Ross protested, looking horrified.

"The trouble with wooden looseboxes is they get hot in the summer and you have to creosote them all the time," I said, not listening to Katie who was howling because Ross had torn up her card.

"Mel, what are you going on about?" Blake had just walked in from riding Colorado, with a sweaty saddle and bridle slung over his arm.

But none of us had time to explain because

we had a visitor and it wasn't someone who was welcome.

"Talk of the devil," Ross said under his breath.

"Bad pennies will keep turning up." Blake bristled.

Mr Richardson swaggered into the yard with his son trailing after him. He had his face set as hard as rock and made me feel positively queasy.

"You owe me two hundred and fifty pounds," he demanded, not beating about the bush. "You've got the nag, now pay up."

Ross looked as if someone had punched him in the stomach. This was the last thing we expected. Of all the nerve . . .

"Where I come from we don't welsh on deals," Mr Richardson added.

"No, you just work your horses to death and then leave them for dead." Blake glowered.

"If I don't get my money I could send some very nasty people round to collect it," Mr Richardson threatened.

"Go jump," Blake said, not moving an inch.

"I'm warning you . . ." Mr Richardson took a step forward.

"And I'm warning you." Blake lowered his voice. "You're a miserable little worm and you're not getting a penny out of us. Now clear off."

"Come on, Dad, let's do as he says."

"Over my dead body. If you won't give me the money I'll take the nag. Now where is he?"

Mr Richardson started looking in all the stables one by one. I could hear Jakey shuffling around and sounding nervous – the last thing I wanted was him getting upset.

"Can't you just leave him alone?" I shouted. "Haven't you done enough damage already?" I was so angry I barely recognized my own voice. "For heaven's sake, the poor pony's got a bad heart. Can't you just let him end the rest of his days in peace?"

I was shaking like a leaf and my eyes were prickling with tears.

Slowly Mr Richardson's son put his hands together and started clapping. "She's right, Dad. And it's about time someone stood up to you."

Mr Richardson glowed red like a beetroot. His nose looked so inflated I thought it was going to explode. For what seemed like an eternity he just stood there glaring at me and then without saying a word he turned on his heel and marched off down the drive.

"Wow!" Ross said, breathing a sigh of relief and looking at me in a new light. "Remind me never to get on the wrong side of you!"

Jakey poked his black and white head over his door as if to check that the coast was clear. I'm sure he had recognized Mr Richardson's voice. I stroked his wrinkled nose, which we had smeared with Vaseline to soften the skin. It had taken ages to clean his whiskers which were stiff with dirt from where he kept falling down. Katie had suggested chopping them off, but horses need whiskers to feel their way around. They are a sort of antennae. "It's OK, boy, he's gone – you're safe!"

James had confirmed that Jakey's knees were badly rheumatic and it was important to take him for gentle walks to loosen the joints. We'd also put him on cod liver oil and Sarah had sent off for a copper bangle which was supposed to work wonders and was specially designed for horses to fit round the top of their knee.

I was just about to fetch Jakey's headcollar to walk him round the yard when Sarah came whizzing up the drive in our old Volvo which sounded as if the exhaust had fallen off yet again. She scrambled out of the passenger door (the driver's door was stuck) and ran across to us, waving a bottle of Asti Spumante in the air.

"I've got it," she cried out excitedly. "I've got the loan!"

Katie whooped in delight and I closed my eyes and whispered, "Thank you, God."

"Charles Stonehouse – eat your heart out!" Sarah yelled, jigging around like a Morris dancer.

It was like a dream come true. We all knew that without grazing we couldn't properly expand the sanctuary. We'd never talked about this in great depth because we didn't want to face the prospect of having to turn horses away and maybe even having to close down. Now we didn't have to worry – our future was assured.

"I hereby christen this Hollywell land," Ross said, standing in the middle of a seven-acre field filled with winter corn and bordering our land. We'd clambered over a wooden stile in the hedge, carrying six glasses and the bottle of bubbly, and Sarah said if anyone saw us they'd think we were mad.

"They think that already," Ross joked, and Blake popped the cork, which flew off into the corn, and wine fizzed out all over the place, showering Katie and catching the arm of my coat.

Danny stuck a stick in the ground and Katie said we should have a special Hollywell flag.

"We've bought thirty acres of land, not climbed Mount Everest," Ross remarked.

"What am I missing out on?" a voice boomed from the gap in the hedge. Rocky stood grinning at us, looking superb in his black leather jacket which said "Rocky – The Return" on the back in gold letters. He'd given us all one for Christmas and Ross and I were the envy of our school.

"You can't be serious?" Sarah said as we all clambered through the corn to join him.

"Never been more serious in my life," Rocky said, putting his hand on his heart and winking at Danny who was goggle-eyed.

Rocky had just been talking to Dom on the telephone. Cassandra had had a brainwave and she was going crazy with excitement. She wanted some of our horses in the studio!

"It would drive the viewers wild," Dom insisted. "Just what the programme needs."

We were all thrown into turmoil.

We eventually decided on Colorado because he was used to bright lights and an audience and Queenie because she was partially deaf and she didn't bat an eyelid at anything. She had appeared with Rocky on stage at his concert and if she could cope with that she could cope with *The Breakfast Bunch*. Besides, she was our lucky mascot.

Jakey and Fluffy were far too weak to be moved and James agreed to come and stay overnight to look after everybody, and so did Mrs Mac, who was a close friend and our leading fund-raiser.

It was so exciting I couldn't believe it was all happening. We were supposed to be staying overnight in a hotel paid for by *The Breakfast Bunch* so we would be in the studio bright and early.

Sarah, Danny, Katie and myself were going with Rocky in the limo and Blake and Ross were going to take the horses in the horsebox. They were to travel through the night, stopping off at various points to give the horses a rest.

Blake polished frantically at Colorado's brown patches even though he already shone like a conker. For his white bits he dusted in chalk powder and then brushed it out with a body brush. There was no time to set to with the shampoo. We decided to leave Colorado's mane long and flowing and I just dampened it down with the water brush, but I plaited Queenie, who looked so pretty with her mane done up, but I rather overdid it with the hairspray so that the eleven neat little buds set like rock. Blake plaited her tail and it looked fantastic.

We set off in the limo that evening and I couldn't stop worrying about Jakey and Fluffy. Sarah said they were in the best of hands with James, and I had to agree.

With Rocky's driving we arrived in London in no time at all and found the hotel straight away. Rocky had stayed there before.

It was huge with masses of corridors and the rooms were like nothing I'd ever seen. The beds were enormous and there was a minibar with every soft drink imaginable, and bars of chocolate, which Katie and Danny polished off in no time.

We went downstairs for a meal and most of *The Breakfast Bunch* were already there waiting for us. Cassandra looked extremely businesslike and well organized, totally different from when she'd stayed at Hollywell. Dom introduced us to the presenters and handed us a green script which had our names written down under Get This!

My knees were shaking like never before.

"Isn't that Harry Enfield who just walked past?" Sarah was peeping at the next table through a vine plant. "I'm sure I've just seen Philip Schofield."

We sat down to eat – chicken and chips and lots of onion rings – and Dom explained how they'd been rehearsing all day and the lady presenter had stormed off in a huff because nobody would take her seriously.

Dom looked really tired and even his bow tie seemed to have wilted. He told us that the Head of Children's Television was at the next table and he had to pull off a good show tomorrow or else. I suddenly realized just how pressurized a job in television could be.

We climbed into bed much later than we'd intended and all I could think of was what if I dried up on set? It had happened on radio so why not on television? What if I made a complete fool of myself?

Within seconds Katie was snoring her head off

and I wished I could have some of her boundless confidence.

I went to sleep thinking about Blake and Ross in the horsebox trundling up the motorway with Queenie and Colorado. We were just hours away from one of the biggest days of our lives . . . And somehow I was determined not to blow it.

"Where's my four-leaf clover?" Katie yelled.

"I can't find my script." Sarah hurled papers in all directions.

"Mel, will you get a move on." Ross looked as white as a sheet and Blake was having trouble with Colorado who was dancing all over the place and threatening to knock over one of the cameras.

Sarah and I had just come out of the Green Room which was where everybody gathered before they went on set. I presume it was called the Green Room because everyone turned pea green with nerves. We'd left it full of shrieking mothers who were there to support their children in *The Breakfast Bunch* talent contest. The way they were carrying on, anybody would think they were the star attraction. A red-haired girl whizzed past me, dressed up as a giant egg and followed by three toddlers in Easter Bunny costumes. Dom had insisted on an Easter theme despite Cassandra's reservations, but already the box-load of Easter eggs which were supposed to be given out at the end of the show had been raided by one of the school choirs. There were bits of silver foil all over the stage where Get This! and Rocky were supposed to perform. Talking about Rocky, where was he?

Cassandra floated by, grasping a clipboard, and Dom followed her, looking wretched and exhausted and clinging on to an Easter Bunny with freckles and blond hair who had just tried to unplug all the cameras.

"Never work with kids and animals," Dom said. "Why do I get the feeling this is going to be a total disaster?"

The Head of Children's Television hovered in the background like some predatory bird and I truly felt sorry for Dom.

"So where is Rocky?" Sarah barked, looking grey with nerves and her red hair clashing with her flushed face.

"Aren't you supposed to be in Make-up?" One of the presenters came up, looking tight-lipped and crippled in an even tighter pair of leather trousers.

We'd completely forgotten.

The make-up artist flung some blusher on my cheeks with the speed of light and Ross squirmed in his chair as he was coated with thick foundation.

Apparently everybody had to wear make-up because of the bright lights, otherwise they looked washed out and ill. I thought it would take more than make-up to make us look healthy. Danny hadn't said a word since breakfast and my stomach felt like a cement mixer.

"Darling, just hang loose, chill out, be cool." One of the presenters was trying to reassure the girl in the giant egg costume, but how she expected her to stay cool under all that inflated rubber I'll never know.

"Of course Felicity has always been a natural." One of the mothers had sneaked into the make-up room and was hounding the presenter.

"Ten minutes before you're on," a researcher told us.

The programme had already started and the talent contest was under way. I just wanted to get back to Queenie and Colorado, who were waiting in the outer studio along with Blake.

"Get This! are in the Green Room," Katie shrieked, pulling out her autograph book and about to dash off.

Suddenly there was a huge crash outside the door.

Rocky walked in, looking so relaxed it was enviable. "Hi, guys, having a nice time?"

The mother talking to the presenter let out a

bloodcurdling scream and the girl in the costume slipped in blind panic, bounced on to her side and couldn't get back up.

"She was lonely," Rocky said. "It was all Blake's idea."

Sarah was gaping like a fish. "This time, Rocky, you've gone too far!"

He'd got Isabella on the end of a leadrope!

But there was no time to argue. The researcher raced up to us, pink and sweating, and dragged us off to the studio. Someone else fiddled with some microphones which fixed on to our jumpers and plonked us down on a multicoloured sofa.

"Where are the phones?" the presenter hissed.

I tried to remember what Dom had told us: sit as still as possible; don't move your heads; keep smiling even when the camera isn't on you. And don't all talk at once. What was he asking for, a miracle?

"Thirty seconds to go," someone said but I was too nervous to notice who. "Stand by for action."

The presenter had a last quick look at her script.

The lights were turned up. Camera three moved into position. The Autocue started rolling . . . We were on air!

Chapter Ten

I'd never been so petrified in my life.

Ross was talking about how the sanctuary got started and he was gradually getting faster and faster. The presenter tried to cut in to suggest moving on to the phones.

"Hello, is that Jason on line two?"

I could hear the presenter asking me a question. I gulped in sheer terror.

Sarah gave me a nudge and I started talking. It was hard to imagine that through that little camera screen thousands of people were watching. I tried to pretend we were just giving a talk and we weren't on television at all. It seemed to work because suddenly everyone was laughing and then I noticed Rocky being dragged on to the set by Isabella, who knocked one of the phones flying and then disappeared up the presenter's skirt. Everyone howled with laughter and there were whoops and whistles from the crew. Suddenly I didn't feel half so nervous.

The special film on Hollywell was brilliant and

made everybody's eyes water, including mine. Then there were more questions from the phone lines and the studio audience. The presenter introduced Blake, who came forward leading Colorado and Queenie. They both looked so beautiful – a wave of excitement ran through the audience. Even a little boy who'd been picking his nose through the whole interview perked up and paid attention. There were more questions for Rocky and then someone asked Blake if he'd got a girlfriend. Blake turned bright red and even the presenter looked smitten. I felt like punching her on the nose.

Finally the address for the Hollywell Stables Fan Club came up on screen and then a quiz question, with the winner receiving a Hollywell sweatshirt, badge, pen, notebook and mug.

Rocky raced off to perform *Chase the Dream* on stage. The smoke machine billowed out artificial smoke and nearly smothered Queenie, who was up there with him. Luckily she didn't bat an eyelid and down in the audience everyone started swaying to the music and joining in the chorus. It was truly a special moment. I could see the credits starting to roll on one of the monitors and then everyone congratulated each other and Dom came running across looking ecstatic.

"Brilliant!" he yelled. "Best show yet! Brilliant!"

The Head of Children's Television shook his

hand and then left by a side door and a lady in a *Breakfast Bunch* T-shirt pushed her way across, brimming with excitement. "The phones are going crazy," she said. "Every line is jammed!"

We scooted back to the Green Room, where Cassandra was opening a bottle of bubbly and pouring it into plastic cups. Pete Jones walked in, looking drop-dead gorgeous and said he would like to join our Fan Club. Katie immediately nabbed him for his autograph.

Ross managed to control Isabella, who had just snaffled away most of the jelly and ice cream laid on for the Easter Bunnies and was about to start on the iced cakes.

"If only all shows ended this way," Dom said, looking wistful and nibbling on a celery stick.

Rocky swept in carrying a huge tray of mini Easter eggs and started passing them round. One of the Easter Bunnies was sick and Isabella was banned from the room after upsetting the soft drinks.

"Here's to *Chase the Dream* and Hollywell Stables!" Cassandra bellowed, looking slightly tipsy and clinging on to Rocky's arm for support. "And to a new Number One!"

We never really considered the possibility of *Chase*

the Dream going to Number One, not seriously anyway. But after our appearance on *The Breakfast Bunch* it seemed to catch the imagination of the whole country.

It was incredible. We received letters and donations from as far away as John O'Groats and the Isle of Wight. The postman had to bring our mail in the back of his car because there was so much of it. Sarah said if we received any more she'd start dreaming about envelopes and we'd have to find a full-time secretary.

"I don't know whether I like being famous," Katie moaned, taking the phone off the hook because it wouldn't stop ringing.

"Enjoy it while it lasts," Rocky advised, "because, believe me, a few months down the road and it will all be forgotten."

Jakey and Fluffy were doing really well. Fluffy's whippet-like body had already started to fill out and he and Jigsaw had become the best of friends.

James had given Jakey a worming powder which would hopefully clear out his system and had taken away some of his droppings to be analysed. His worm count was found to be far too high – the chances are he hadn't been wormed for years. It was a routine task which we did with all our horses every six weeks without fail.

Jakey's heartbeat was now much stronger and, provided he had a quiet, easy life, there was no reason why he shouldn't live for a few more years. The main thing was he now seemed to have the will to carry on. He was always the first in the morning to be looking out over his stable door and he had the appetite of an African elephant. Sarah said at this rate he'd be a roly-poly in no time at all.

"Give me this kind of life any day," Blake said as we both leaned over Jakey's door, watching him devour his extra-large haynet.

I knew exactly what he meant. All the television stuff was exciting and fun but we'd been glad to get back to Hollywell. It was the horses which mattered the most.

"Here, I didn't have a chance to give this to you earlier."

Blake pushed something into my hand, tightly wrapped in tissue paper and still warm from his pocket.

"What's this?" I said, totally taken by surprise.

Blake and I were especially close friends – I could talk to him about anything – but he'd never given me a present before, not since Christmas anyway.

117

"Open it and see."

I gently unfolded the pink tissue paper, trying not to let my hands tremble. Inside was a box with gold hinges on one side.

"Well, go on, open it."

I eased open the box and inside was a tiny bronze figure of a Shetland pony rolling.

"It was the nearest I could get to Fluffy," Blake said, stroking Jakey's nose. Jakey had heard the tissue rustling and thought it was something to eat.

"Oh, Blake, it's beautiful. It's absolutely gorgeous!"

"Are you two going to stand there all day or what?" Rocky shouted from the back door, wearing Sarah's flowery pinny and beating something in a plastic jug. "Come on, the charts are about to start!"

It was four o'clock on a Sunday afternoon and Bruno Brookes was giving the Top Forty rundown. This was the moment we'd all been waiting for!

What I couldn't understand was why Rocky preferred to hear the news on the radio rather than ring up his manager. Apparently most artists did this because it was more exciting. To me it just seemed to prolong the agony and I didn't think my nerves could stand it.

Rocky was skittering around like a cat on hot bricks, insisting on keeping busy by whipping up a low-fat chocolate cake. He'd decided to go on a diet since Poison Pandora had commented that he'd got a middle-age paunch.

"Rocky, can't you just go and ring your manager and be done with it?" Sarah pleaded.

"And break with years of tradition?" Rocky looked horrified.

Katie clung on to her lucky four-leaf clover, which had had so much wear in the last few months it was falling to pieces.

Bruno introduced a new entry at thirty-seven which sounded like a cat screeching.

"Not long now," Rocky said, beating harder at the cake mixture, which was flicking all over the walls.

"Only another thirty-six records!" Blake grinned.

"I can't bear it," Katie yelled, curling up in Jigsaw's basket with the tea towel draped over her head.

Danny turned up the radio when it got to Number Twenty-five, which was a heavy metal record and it practically shook the kitchen walls.

Sarah made gallons of tea and then forgot to pour it out until it was almost black. Rocky flung the cake mixture into a tin and slammed it in the oven and Sarah said he'd knocked all the air out of it. He then proceeded to pour himself a mug of tea and mixed in six spoonfuls of sugar without thinking.

"I'm fine, really I am," he said, gulping at the tea and not even noticing the sugar.

Fluffy looked at us all as if we were mad.

Suddenly the charts jumped to Number Seventeen and Rocky said blow to his diet and ripped open a packet of chocolate biscuits.

"If that Pandora's at Number One I'll die," Sarah said as a romantic ballad drifted over the airwaves but did little to soothe anyone's nerves.

"We're into the Top Ten!" Rocky shouted, repeating Bruno Brookes word for word. "Who's that at Number Seven?"

The tension was unbearable.

"I can't take much more of this," Sarah whimpered.

Number Five was a modern version of the Can-Can and, with Jigsaw barking after them, Katie and Danny insisted on dancing round the kitchen, looking more as if they were doing a version of the Highland Fling than anything remotely resembling the Can-Can.

"Ssssh, ssssh." Rocky turned up the volume to full blast.

"And now for the moment we've all been waiting for." Bruno's voice was bristling with suspense. "At Number Two . . ."

If this was Pandora we were home and clear. Rocky would be at Number One. But if it wasn't . . .

The gentle lull of *Snowflake* throbbed out of the radio.

"We've done it!" Rocky yelled, going bananas. "We've gone and done it!" He whooped for joy.

Ross swirled me round and Sarah brushed at her eyes with the back of her hand.

Rocky was at Number One!

"I can't take it in," he spluttered, his cheeks suddenly wet with tears.

Chase the Dream had gone all the way, just as he'd predicted. Hollywell Stables was at Number One.

Dom and Cassandra were on the phone straight away to congratulate us. Rocky couldn't speak because he was feeling too emotional. Sarah said it was *The Breakfast Bunch* viewers who had made all the difference – they'd all gone out and bought the record.

Blake reached for the champagne bottle and Rocky popped the cork just as *Chase the Dream* came over the airwaves. My hands were trembling so much I could hardly hold my glass.

"To Rocky and to Hollywell," Sarah toasted, and we all knew this was a very special moment.

"I still can't believe it," Rocky said, blowing his

nose on the tissue Blake had passed him.

"Dreams really can come true," Katie stated.

"Only if you believe in them hard enough," I added.

"You realize life will never be quite the same again, don't you?" Sarah said.

And how could it be with Fluffy, Jakey and Isabella as the latest residents at Hollywell?